# TALIA SUROVA

# WARM
# ME
# UP

<u>Other Works by Talia Surova:</u>
*Draw Me In (Greenpoint Artists* prequel novella)
*Hold Me Tight (Greenpoint Artists* Book One)
Call Me Saffron (connected to *Greenpoint Artists*
series)
*What's Yours is Mine*

www.TaliaSurova.com
talia@taliasurova.com

For Dan
Always, but especially this time

# Chapter One

It still wasn't right. Sure, she'd captured the dark slash of his eyebrows well enough, the sharp curves of cheekbones, the powerful stance as he stood, braced against a clear cerulean sky, haloed by the sun. But the haunted look in his eyes? How could brown flecks of paint on canvas convey something like that?

And yet she had to try. The dream image was stuck in her brain, lingering behind her eyes, playing on endless repeat. More vivid than real life.

Like the three dreams before it.

And like the three dreams before it, if she didn't paint it, didn't pour the images onto the canvas, didn't get it right—she couldn't move on.

Stupid dreams. Stupid, disruptive, troubling, compelling dreams.

Maybe it wasn't the eyes. Maybe it was the light across his face, the dappling of brown and pink. A slant of shadow across his eyes suggesting inner pain…

Georgette Soren glanced at the wall clock in the art studio. She had time. Ten minutes, maybe even twenty. Then she'd clean up and head out. She dipped her paintbrush in the ochre smear on her palette, swished it lightly in the tin of turpentine beside her easel, and dove back into the dream.

Shadows across the eyes, yes. It worked. Now for the hair. And his shirt, gray-green with a faded logo. Tricky to get right. She could see it in her head...

Time passed. She forgot to check the clock. Nothing mattered, nothing existed but this.

Someone rapped on the door. "Georgette! I know you're in there!" Sam's voice.

*Oh God.* Sam. What time was it?

She practically ran to the studio door and hastily unlocked it. "I'm so sorry! I can't believe I missed the show!" It was at a coffeehouse, and Sam's band was playing background music, but still. She'd always gone to his performances. "The time got away from me. Did anyone get a video? I'll be there tomorrow night, I promise." She reached out to him, but he practically shoved her away, stalking past her to the wet canvas.

He stared down at it, his eyebrows knotted, anger and puzzlement clear on his face. "What the hell, Georgette?"

"I had to get it out of my head. I lost track of the time."

He whirled around and gazed down at her from his great gawky height. Six foot two, all wire and sinew and deep brown skin. He smelled like bubble gum. "You're not the woman I fell for."

"I'm only—"

But he was on a roll. "That one cared about me.

She listened to me. She made me feel like everything was under control. You've turned into this obsessed lunatic. I don't recognize you anymore." He smeared the painting with his finger, then wiped the paint off on his jeans.

Georgette fought the impulse to rush over and fix the damage. It would only set Sam off.

Usually when he got upset, she knew the right words to soothe him. She was good at analyzing his underlying trauma, easing his discomfort. But usually he wasn't mad at her.

Their relationship wasn't like that. *She* wasn't like that.

Usually. "I know, it's weird. I don't feel like myself." And it was true. "Ever since the first dream, I —"

"Who is he?" His caustic voice sliced past her words, cutting her off. "Are you sleeping with him?"

Georgette winced. "Like I keep telling you, he doesn't exist. Dr. Wamsutter says—"

"I thought you stopped seeing that lamebrain excuse for a therapist after this started."

"I did. But the dreams haven't gone away."

"Dreams, my ass." Sam grabbed the painting and tossed it on the paint-spattered cement floor.

Georgette rushed for it, but it was too late. The image was irreparably damaged, the colors melting into each other, the lines blurred.

She knelt on the floor, staring at her destroyed work, and swallowed hard to stop herself from crying.

Sam gazed down at her. "You don't love me, do you? You love *him*." He pointed at the painting. "You show more passion for those damned paintings than you've ever shown for me."

"Love? I don't love him. I can't. He doesn't exist."

"And me? How do you feel about me?"

Once, her relationship with Sam had made her feel in control. Had made her feel useful. Had fit neatly into her life too.

When she'd made a list before moving in with him, the pros had outweighed the cons. He lived in lower Manhattan, a straight-shot bus ride from her grad school. He was hooked into the music scene, so they always had something interesting to do on a Saturday night. He leaned on her, and she loved feeling needed. Georgette and Sam as a pair had made sense.

She looked up at him, blinking away unexpected tears. "This isn't working, is it? Us. We're not good for each other anymore." Being with him didn't make her feel safe. Nothing did.

As any self-respecting hipster musician with a trust fund should, Sam lived in the far East Village.

Carrying a heavy duffel bag filled with her most important possessions, Georgette tripped down five flights, her calves aching by the time she reached street level, and stepped outside.

The cold December air slapped her like a rebuke. She hurried along the crowded sidewalk, dodging lollygaggers deciding which farm-to-table restaurant to dine in tonight or looking for the latest gourmet donut shop. She wouldn't miss living here.

Oh, who was she kidding? She'd miss it like crazy. It was full of energy, even if it was overpriced, overprivileged energy. Walking down Sam's block, crossing the street, walking down the next block, Georgette scanned the crowd as she went. That guy might be a young investment banker, full of himself because he was living the bohemian life. That woman probably had a day job working in a shoe store and lived with five roommates in a studio walkup. That guy —

Georgette stopped dead.

That guy didn't exist.

He looked exactly like the man she'd painted, the one from her dreams.

Impossible. But here.

He was walking past, moving quickly.

She must have imagined the similarity. Must have. Sure, the overall shape was the same as the man in her dreams—high cheekbones and a long chin. His hair color was the same too, a dark brown shot with the red-tinted threads of someone who spent a lot of time in the sun. But that was all. That had to be all.

She rushed to catch up, to see that face again. When he stopped at a streetlight, she'd catch another glimpse of his face. Then she'd know for sure.

He was half a block ahead, walking with a long, easy stride. She hefted her duffel over her shoulder and hurried.

He turned the corner. She ran, the heavy bag smacking against her side, and felt more than a little foolish.

When she got to the corner, she peered ahead but saw no well-built man with dark hair wearing a leather bomber jacket. He was gone. Or, more likely, he hadn't existed. Her distracted brain had conjured him up.

She stumbled to the bus stop and sat on the chilled metal bench, glancing around despite herself as she waited. He must be blocks away by now. Still, after she boarded the bus and settled into a seat by the window, she checked outside one more time. Just in case.

The door to the fancy café swung open. A man stepped out.

It was him.

This time she got a good look at his face. The line

of his nose, the height of his forehead, the slope of his chin. Every detail.

It was the man from her paintings. The man who didn't exist.

Somehow, he seemed to sense her gaze, even through the thick bus window. He looked up. He saw her.

He reacted.

His mouth opened slightly, his eyebrows shot up. He said something. Something that looked an awful lot like "Georgette?"

# Chapter Two

Alanna looked up from her easel when Georgette came into their shared studio space. "Georgie! I didn't know you were coming today. I thought you were busy with end-of-semester crap."

"No, I—" Georgette's voice cracked, and she couldn't finish the sentence. She set her duffel on the floor by the door, and tried again to speak normally, like someone who hadn't seen an impossible person. "I thought I'd drop my stuff off. Here, I mean. I went to —I saw Sam. I picked up some of my things, and he came in while I was there. I thought—" But she couldn't get the words out. *That man.* His gaze so direct, his expression sharpening as he saw her. His response to her.

Alanna came over, still holding her paintbrush. "You okay? Did it stir up stuff? I'm no psychologist in training, not like you, but I know it's not normal to feel nothing about—"

"I saw him."

"Yeah, you said. I'm sorry. That must have been hard. I thought he wasn't going to be around today."

"Not Sam. Him." Georgette went over to her recent set of paintings, stacked up and leaning against the wall. Six paintings. She flipped through them. The one of his face full frame, the image taken from that first drawing, that first dream. The one of him crouched in a barren space, clutching his head, anguished. The one of him sitting alone on a subway bench on an empty platform, looking desolate. The one of him standing on a cliff edge, outlined against a stark blue sky, his arms wide, his head flung back, ecstatic, and its companion piece: same cliff edge, but seen from below as he peered down at the viewer, his expression clouded with dismay. The one of his body on the ground, surrounded by menacing skyscrapers.

Alanna had followed her over. "Him? But…"

"I *know*."

Alanna put down the paintbrush on Georgette's easel stand. "Tell all."

Georgette set the final painting into place along the wall and stepped back to stand by her friend. Not many, in the end. Just the six. Six vivid, peculiar dreams. Six paintings created in an obsessed frenzy. Even looking at them made her blush with the remembered thrill of creation. He'd felt so real, so immediate. So intimately hers.

"It makes sense that he's a real person. They're too specific not to be. I mean, look at this." Alanna, Georgette's petite blonde studio mate and best friend, pointed to a mole on the painted cheek in one picture, a black beauty spot enhancing the slash of cheekbone. "And you painted him at different ages too." She gestured at the ones of him standing against a cliff edge. "He's got to be a teenager here." And then at the one on the subway platform. "But clearly not here. Is he that hot in real life?"

"Alanna! That is *so* not the point."

Her friend grinned, impish. "Just wondered."

It didn't make sense. "If he's real, that means I know him, right? I mean, he said my name. Unless I imagined that. How could I know him this well"— Georgette gestured toward the paintings—"and not know that I know?"

"You're the psychologist. You tell me."

What would her professors say? She ticked off the possibilities on her fingers. "Hallucination. Which rarely happens, only under the influence of certain psychedelics or specific psychoses. Daydream. But I'd know. I was awake. I'm sure I was."

"What else?"

"Projection, because I desperately want something to be so. Which seems the most likely, doesn't it? I mean, I'd just left Sam's place, and he's not a happy guy right now. So instead of dwelling on the pain our breakup caused him, I chose to picture this mysterious stranger. It's not such a stretch to hypothesize that I conjured up the entire encounter based on the shape of a man's chin and curl of his hair."

Alanna regarded her. "Or maybe he's real."

A shiver ran through Georgette. It felt like a premonition, but that was nonsense.

Alanna went over to one of the paintings and stroked her finger along the ragged edge of the stretched canvas. "If it were me, you know what I'd do? I'd go out there and search for the guy. Plant myself at that bus stop and wait. As long as it took. I'd take a picture of one of these paintings with my phone and show it to the waiters in that café. I'd look for him."

Georgette headed to the industrial sink in the corner, its counter littered with brushes and rags. She picked up the last clean mug and poured some water, gulping it down. "That presumes that he's real and that he's going to come back through. And that he's worth meeting." She shook her head. "I've got enough to do, finding a new place to live—"

"You're staying with me."

"For a week or so. Not forever. Plus, I have to finish that report for my fieldwork assignment. And my preliminary dissertation outline. I don't have time to go searching for the man who wasn't there." Georgette rinsed out the mug and set it down. "It's just a weird coincidence. One of those random things. Very New York, if you think about it. Some guy I've never met who happens to look similar to this." She waved her arm, encompassing the paintings. "And who said something that I misinterpreted to be my name. Classic. Everyone thinks the world revolves around themselves. I should write a paper on that."

She avoided looking at the paintings. She was being practical. Down-to-earth. Realistic, the way her mother had taught her. Keeping her emotions reined in, not letting herself spin out of control. She needed that, for her own sanity. She'd learned that lesson ten years ago.

No, her dream man didn't exist, even if he did have a doppelgänger out there wandering the city. "What do you say we grab dinner? Any chance Miles is cooking?" Alanna's boyfriend was a great cook.

Alanna made a face. "He says we've got too much work. Claims Jared's taking on too many clients too fast, and we can't make it work. In fact, Miles thinks we need to pull an all-nighter tonight." Then she smiled, transforming her face from serious woman to mischievous little girl. "But he's wrong. It'll be two hours, tops, unless he goes into professional worry mode. So I've got a surprise for him. I'm going to show up at his apartment in my red leather bustier. We'll see how long this shampoo ad mock-up takes us then."

"That man doesn't know how good he has it."

Alanna grinned. "Oh, I think he knows."

Before they left the studio, Georgette glanced back

at the paintings of her mystery man, as if looking again would reveal hidden truths. Which was ridiculous. She'd painted him herself, after all. And yet those dark eyes gazing from the multiplicity of canvases burned through her, leaving her shaken.

She shut the door and followed her friend downstairs.

Alanna's apartment was spookily quiet. Alanna had gone off to her all-nighter with Miles. Her brother aka business partner aka roommate Jared had floated in, bearing pierogis and poppy-seed strudel from the local Polish deli, inhaled a huge serving, then disappeared into his bedroom.

Georgette pulled up the third page of short-term apartment listings on craigslist and stared at the offerings. One in Park Slope. Pretty neighborhood, but so family oriented, she'd need a stroller as an accessory. Plus, anything affordable had to be the size of a walk-in closet. Another in Canarsie. She'd need a gun for that one. And body armor. And mace.

The one in Staten Island might be worth a look. A hellish commute, but at least she could afford it.

"You don't want to live in Staten Island." Jared had popped back into the living room and now hovered over her shoulder, reading the listings. "We'll never see you. You might as well be in Idaho." He shuddered.

"And how will you get to school? The ferry? In mid-February when the wind chill is minus three hundred and it's sleeting out?"

She closed the browser window and raised her eyebrows at his attire. He looked sharp in a bright yellow shirt with a pencil-thin leather tie. "I didn't realize the dress code was so formal around here. I'd better change."

He grinned at her. "I'm going to a Kickshaw Films party. Want to come?"

"I'm not a party girl."

"They have great food. And movie stars."

"Is that why you're going?"

"I'm drumming up business." With a flourish, he revealed a glossy business card in his hand, like a magician presenting a magic trick.

Georgette laughed. "Admit it, you're going for the fancy drinks."

He grinned. "That too."

After he grabbed a clashing orange wool coat and left, she clicked on the craigslist page to refresh it, but the listings blurred together.

The apartment was too quiet. Not even the noisy neighbors upstairs were home. No clunking footsteps, no scraping of furniture. Dead quiet in midwinter, and not even her own home.

She closed the computer and grabbed her winter

coat. There was one place that felt like home these days. The creative impulse was bone-deep, humanity's solace against the dark. Why not make it hers?

It had nothing to do with wanting to see that face on her canvases again. The face she'd projected onto some stranger this afternoon. Absolutely nothing. Because that would be impractical, illogical, and not grounded in reality. And Georgette Soren was always grounded in reality.

Always.

When she got to the studio, the first thing Georgette did was restack the canvases of her dream guy. Then, for good measure, she threw a tarp over them. She didn't want him staring at her reproachfully from out of the canvas. He had no right to make her feel guilty. It wasn't her fault he wasn't real.

Then she put on some soft jazz, set a new canvas on her easel, and tried to paint one of her usual abstracts, with swirls and peaceful swaths of color like a faded sunset sky. But somehow it turned into a strong nose, dark slashes of eyebrows, puzzled eyes.

Nothing for it but to wipe the painting with a turpentine-dipped rag and start again. Sam was right. It was unnatural to be obsessed like this.

Oops, there it was again. A slice of cheek, starkly curved. And that could be a hand, gesturing in the air.

Calling out to someone?

Someone on a bus?

A knock at the door made her jump and smear the canvas with a jagged brushstroke. She turned, gripping the wooden brush handle like a weapon.

The door creaked open, and a familiar face appeared. Finn McKenna of Finn's Fermentation Factory, the industrial kitchen that took up the lower two floors. Landlord and friend. He had an apron on over his jeans and smelled strongly of vinegar.

"Oh! Finn. I thought I was alone in the building." Georgette lowered the brush, feeling foolish. What would she have done, anyway? *Painted* the intruder to death? "Weren't you supposed to go on vacation with Raven and the kids?"

He ran a hand through his unruly mess of light brown hair. "Yeah, until Roman asked me for some catering advice. Next thing I knew, he'd roped me into making my special new recipes to unveil at his party." Finn's friend Roman ran a wildly popular New York culture blog called *Roman Del Valle Knows Best*. His extravagant praise for Finn's pickles had a lot to do with the success of the Fermentation Factory. Of course Finn felt some loyalty. "And then of course I had to come up with the special new recipes." He proffered a plate. "I was hoping you could taste test."

As Georgette plucked a seaweed-wrapped kimchi

ball from the plate, Finn's cell phone rang. He fished it out of his apron pocket and answered it. "I know, I'm late. Yeah, I lost track, how'd you guess?" He had a smile in his voice. It must be his wife on the phone. "Yeah, I do think it's good. Georgette's trying it out."

She nodded enthusiastically as the sweet-salty tang burst in her mouth.

"She likes it. No, it's still fermenting. Tomorrow, I promise. Okay." He clicked off. "Raven sends her love and says to get my ass home. Thanks for being my test subject. Don't stay too late. They're saying it might snow."

"Yes, Dad." Finn was a nurturer by nature. He liked feeding and caring for people. Unlike her own parents, who always seemed like they were playacting the part of warm caregivers, Finn was the real thing.

Georgette shook off the thought and said goodbye to Finn. She set the plate down by the easel and dipped her brush back into the paint.

Then she looked at the painting. It clearly wanted to be a representational work. Who was she to stand in the way?

Half an hour later—or was it two hours?—the painting was shaping up. Thick blue slanted lines representing the bus window, a scratched glass surface. Behind it, a stark Byronic face—broad forehead, sharp slope of nose. Just the shapes, still rough, but there.

A sharp rapping interrupted the flow, overlaying the beat of the music.

She painted some more, dimly aware of the sound.

Again, a rapping sound.

Someone at the door? Shades of Sam's visit two weeks ago. Maybe it was him again.

No. It was coming from the window.

Three floors above the street, and someone was knocking on the window.

# Chapter Three

When James had gotten the art studio address an hour ago, he'd felt compelled to get on the subway and come straight over. But now that he was standing on the street staring at the oversized Finn's Fermentation Factory sign, it felt like the dead end it probably was. The warehouse was dark. The entire short block was dark, for that matter, with shadowed artistic graffiti-painted walls leading to the East River. Desolate and empty. Why would Georgette be in her studio now? At nine p.m. a week before Christmas? She was probably at a party. Or out with friends. Or home, wherever that was.

Still, the third-floor windows were lit. Maybe someone had forgotten to turn off the lights.

Or maybe someone was up there.

The sharp December wind sliced through him. He didn't relish the long walk back to the subway. And what if Georgette *was* up there?

The small door next to the truck bay was locked. James tried the handle to be sure. There was no bell, so he pounded on the door. No response. But if Georgette was all the way up there, how could she hear him down here?

He gazed up at the tantalizing third floor. It wasn't

that far, not for an experienced climber. Of course, without grappling hooks or rocky outcroppings, it wouldn't be easy.

Unless…

He walked around to the side of the building. Sure enough, a fire escape. But the ladder was retracted and out of reach.

With a running start, he launched himself at the wall. The trick was speed. Not stopping. Not thinking. Just doing. He ran up the wall, his momentum carrying him the few steps he needed, and grabbed on to the bottom of the ironwork fire escape. Then he made his way, hand over hand, to the edge. Brushing against the useless ladder, he hauled himself up and over onto the overhang. Heart beating, cheeks flushed, feeling every bit the city adventurer. He'd needed this. Too much time in the city made him stir-crazy.

He tried to stand, but the sleeve of his coat caught on the protruding ladder and yanked his arm back. He was stuck.

Fine. There was an easy solution. He shed the coat. Barely feeling the chill, he climbed the rest of the way up the fire escape and peeked in the window.

A floor lamp flared in the center of a large studio space, illuminating a cement floor splattered with paint, stacks of canvases along three walls, and an array of large, spiky sculptures along the fourth wall. There was an industrial sink in the corner and a large rack with art supplies next to it.

There was a woman in the room, over by the side wall. She painted on an easel-mounted canvas with furious brushstrokes, as if possessed by the spirit of the work. Her hair was the right shade of brown, but it was pulled back into a tight ponytail, and he couldn't tell its texture. She wore a paint-smeared smock, obscuring her figure, and her face was in the shadows.

But he knew. He could tell from her stance, from the curve of her elbows and the pace of her movements. It was her. His Georgette.

He rapped on the window. She paused, then rubbed her nose with the back of her hand and resumed painting.

He rapped harder. *Turn. Look. See me.*

The wind sweeping down the street stung his shoulder, his cheek. Damn, it was cold out here. He was coming down from the adrenaline high.

He knocked again.

She stopped painting.

He tapped once more.

She glanced over at the door.

*No, over here!*

His knuckles were getting sore by the time she finally turned toward the window. She was still lovely, her face that perfect Modigliani oval, but grown up now, fully formed. And so self-contained, though maybe that was because someone was rapping at her window.

With the dark behind him, the light inside, she probably couldn't see his face yet. But as she came closer, she would. And then...

She stopped dead. Frowned deep. And then...

She smacked her cheeks hard, wincing at the impact. He winced with her.

Her hands came away from her face. She'd left a blue smear high along one cheekbone.

And still she stood there staring at him.

He started shivering. Dried sweat against the back of his neck prickled with icy foreboding. "Open the window!" Could she hear him? "It's freezing out here!"

She peered out through the closed window at him. "Who are you?"

*What?* "James! It's James! Can I come in?"

Still she hesitated.

There was a man outside the studio window. Not just any man. *Him. He* was out there. On the fire escape. As if he'd stepped out of her canvas and—

She glanced over at the half-finished painting. The image of his face—the same face—was still there, the wet paint glistening under the studio light.

It made no sense. But he was real, and he was

shivering. Well, of course. He wore a white button-down shirt, no coat. Not even a hat or scarf. In twenty-degree weather, with a bitter wind coming off the river. Proof he was real. If she was daydreaming him up, she'd put him in an elegant wool coat.

She pried open the window. It stuck, resisting her. When it released, it slid up with startling speed. The man nearly fell into the room.

Georgette took a step back as he straightened up, briskly rubbing his arms.

If she'd thought she'd responded to the man in her dreams, it was nothing compared to the real thing. He radiated masculinity. Even in shirtsleeves, he was clearly muscular, with a confident physicality.

He grinned. "I know what you're thinking. How positively James of me to climb the fire escape in the middle of winter."

*What?*

He gave her a sidelong look, playful but with an edge, as if some strong emotion bubbled under the surface. He obviously expected her to say something, but her brain was electric static and silence.

After a beat, he continued, more somber. "And you'd be right. But I had to see you. Knowing you were here, in New York... We never—after what happened that day, we never saw each other again. I needed to—" He paused, measuring her. The look in his eyes engulfed her, radiating heat and darkness. "Bad idea, I see. Of course it was." His mouth twisted, bitter. "So you hold it against me too, huh? Just like your parents. Should have figured that."

She rubbed her arms, as if chilled skin was contagious. "I don't—I think—I've never met you before." A glance back at her canvas gave the lie to this, but he couldn't see the front of the easel from this angle.

He glared at her. "If you want me to go, say so. Don't pretend you don't remember. That's ludicrous."

"Not pretending." She should say more. She knew she should. Something about happenstance and logic and random similarities. But she couldn't find the words. Couldn't think straight. He was here. Him. And he said he knew her. His presence—his existence —it was too much.

*Past is done.* That was her mantra. *One careful step at a time. No risks. No danger.*

This was…

She didn't know this man. She couldn't. If she'd met him, she'd remember. The guy wasn't easily forgettable, with his loose-limbed grace, his mercurial emotions, and an overwhelming presence that seemed to fill the large studio space as if no man had ever been here before and no man would ever be here again.

"I don't understand, Georgie. Is this some kind of

sick game?"

Georgie. He knew her name.

*He knew her name.*

"No game. I don't remember you." Her heart was beating too fast. Her breath kept hiccupping in her chest. Classic signs of panic. But Georgette never panicked.

*Get hold of yourself. Go about this methodically. Don't freak.* "How did you find me?"

"The guy you—lived?—with. He tagged you on Facebook, in a public post. I looked him up and found his phone number." He came close now, examining her face intently. "You're serious, aren't you? You don't remember me. At all?" He reached out as if he was about to touch her, and she almost wanted him to—but then he abruptly dropped his hand and laced both hands together, as if to circumvent the impulse.

She shook her head, mute. Her voice didn't seem to want to work.

"Nothing about our relationship at all?" He swallowed, clearly shaken by this thought. "Not even making out under the bridge that time my father busted us for loitering?"

She shook her head again. He sounded so sincere, like this had actually happened.

He continued, a thread of desperation in his deep voice. "Or when I accidentally spilled that neon-blue drink on your yellow dress and you dunked me under the water in Kate's pool? That was the day we first kissed." He grinned briefly, a painful smile.

She did have a yellow sundress. And it had a faint blue stain on the skirt, but somehow she hadn't wanted to donate it to Goodwill. It probably still hung in the guest room closet in her parents' home in New Mexico.

Her pulse was tapping a fast rhythm in her throat, the air in the studio felt stifling, and James—this stranger who knew her, had apparently been in love with her—was standing far too close, looking at her far too intently. It was all too much. And still she couldn't seem to think right.

She'd studied temporary dissociation, the feeling of being outside your body, as if the experience was happening to someone else. But she'd never imagined it would feel like this. This shutdown, this stuttering inside her brain.

She took a step back. Then another. "Why did you come? What do you want from me?"

He grabbed her hands in his, stopping her. His skin felt cold against hers, which must be why it sent a shudder through her, because she didn't react this way. Not even to Sam.

It was the surprise. The strangeness. Not a visceral, remembered reaction to his extremely male presence.

An extremely male presence who gripped her hands so hard, it hurt. "Jesus, Georgette. You have to ask?" His voice was a growl, soft and unbearably sexy. "When I saw you through that bus window this morning, I thought I must have gotten hit by a taxi without realizing it and was lying in the street hallucinating you. You don't know..." His voice shook with barely suppressed emotion. "I went to Albuquerque, did you know that? Your parents blocked the door. They said you hated me. That's how I found out you'd come out of the coma. Nice, huh?" His mouth twisted, no humor left. "I've always wondered if you said that, or if it was just them."

He even knew where she'd lived. Knew about her head trauma. This was real. It couldn't be, didn't make sense, because that meant...meant... Her brain stuttered to a stop.

He stroked her cheek with his finger, circled down to her mouth. It was outrageously intimate but she didn't stop him. She breathed in the scent of incipient snow, of salt air, of clean skin. Tantalizingly familiar. He smelled right. How could that be?

"It's always been there, in the back of my mind. I've always wondered what really happened to you. How you really felt. And you're okay, you're whole. Look at you." His gaze kindled, then he went somber. "But you don't remember me. How is that even possible?"

"I don't know." It came out as a whisper, a wisp of a phrase. She felt ensorcelled, as if he were a wizard casting a spell over her, rendering tonight—this entire day—into a bizarre dream.

A dream in which a stranger came into the third-floor walkup via the window ledge. In which they were alone in the building and he was looking at her like he wanted to eat her whole.

God knew what he'd do if he spotted the paintings.

*Oh no.* The paintings. Including the half-finished one on her easel. If he saw it, he'd—

With that thought, her brain sparked into action. She grabbed her paintbrushes and turpentine can. "This has been fascinating. Truly. But I need to get going, and I'm afraid you do too."

He looked baffled. Hurt. "Georgette."

"Seriously. It's been quite an eye-opener." Did she sound as out of breath as she felt? She turned away, toward the sink, before she could betray herself. "Thank you for stopping by. I trust your curiosity has been satisfied, and now you can go on your way. It's good to have closure. I'm sorry I can't tell you anything, but you see, I didn't know about you until tonight." There. She sounded sane. Normal. On point. A bit clinical, but so be it.

"Don't do this. Don't shut me out again."

She turned back toward him, belatedly realizing she was clutching her brushes and tin so hard, the turpentine was nearly sloshing out. "I can't. I can't do this. I just—you came in here and turned everything I know upside down. Do you have any idea what that's like? You have to go. Please." The words, raw and far too true, felt torn from her.

James looked as shaken as she felt. "Well. That's clear enough."

"You did say if I said to go, you would."

He did. Though he hesitated at the door to the stairs, holding the frame, looking back, his expression fierce. "It's not closure, not by a long shot. But it'll have to do."

After he left, the room felt smaller. Darker.

He'd been here. This had happened.

James. She hadn't even gotten his full name, but his roughed-in face gazed from across the room at her from an unfinished canvas, the paint still wet. The same dark eyes, windblown brown hair, sharp curves of cheekbones. The same man.

James. She thought she'd dreamed him into reality, but the truth was even stranger. The truth threatened to unravel her entire life. If he was right, she had a gaping hole in her memory where he'd once been.

How was that possible?

## Chapter Four

The leather bomber jacket hung from the bottom rung of the fire escape, barely out of reach. A profoundly ironic metaphor. He shouldn't have bothered coming here. What had he expected? That she'd want to hash out the events from ten years ago, yeah, maybe. Even better, that she'd embrace him and say, "I'm all better now, stop worrying about me." Something. Not this. Never this. She didn't even remember him. And she seemed so closed, so stern, with mental *Keep Out* signs in flashing neon all around her.

Plus, he'd lost his damned jacket. He'd tried twice and failed both times to reach it.

He took another running leap at the wall but stuttered to a stop halfway up and dropped back down to the sidewalk. No adrenaline, no thrill of excitement to fuel his jump this time.

The lit windows on the third floor mocked his failure. He hoped she wasn't up there watching him.

At least all this running and jumping was warming him up. One more go at it, then he'd give up. Buy another jacket. Leave that damned thing dangling down as a symbol of his forlorn attempt to reconnect with his past.

One and two and run and...

Stub his toe on the stubborn brick wall.

Behind him, someone snorted. "A new form of parkour?"

James whipped around. A guy around his age gave him a cherubic smile and chortled again. He wore an orange wool coat over a bright yellow shirt and a narrow leather tie, his dirty blond hair sticking up in the center in a fifties-style duck wave.

Well, sure. *He* was wearing a coat. He could afford to laugh.

"I'm trying to retrieve my jacket."

The other guy peered up at it. "How'd it get there?"

"I climbed up there earlier. Dropped it on the way up."

The guy's eyebrows shot up. "You didn't think to take the stairs?" He gestured around the corner. "I'm going there now. Maybe I can let you in and you can climb down the fire escape to get the jacket."

An uncomfortable knot formed in his chest. If he didn't know better, he'd say it felt like jealousy. "You're going to visit Georgette? You know her?"

"Is that why you were climbing up there? To see her?" The man frowned at James, his mouth pursed in suspicion. "How well do you know her? Couldn't you just call?"

"I don't have her phone number. We've been out of touch." James was shivering now. Damn, it was cold. "I'm not a stalker. I left when she asked me to, and I'm not going to try to see her again."

The guy tilted his head. "Kicked you out, huh? I'm sensing a story here."

James would have laughed if he didn't feel so much like an icicle. "You could say that."

"Why don't I help you get that jacket down and then you buy me a drink and tell me all about it?"

She'd never noticed before how self-contained her mother's voice mail tone sounded. Professionally soothing, but so detached. "Leave a message, and I'll get back to you as soon as I can. If you need more immediate help, call the hotline."

Georgette hung up. Ten p.m. in Albuquerque. Her mother was probably in bed with her night guard in her mouth, her long hair plaited in pigtail braids, and her flannel sleep mask on the nightstand while she read a thick biography of someone famous who'd died centuries ago. Answering the phone would break her circadian rhythm, she'd say.

Her dad might be downstairs in the den watching *Seinfeld* reruns, but more likely he was in Paris or Istanbul for work again.

Slipping her phone into her painting smock's

ample pocket, Georgette shivered as if the winter wind outside had blown into the loft, making its way into her bloodstream. As if James had transmitted it with his chilled touch.

He'd stroked her cheek, and it had felt more intimate than making love with Sam ever had. And now his face, rough but recognizable, stared at her from the canvas. Mocking her. *Remember me? We were in love.*

She grabbed her paint rag, ready to dip it in turpentine and smear that hauntingly handsome face beyond recognition. Paint a new image on top. Maybe a Christmas wreath in honor of the season, complete with shimmering ornaments and bristly pinecones. Something cheery and bright, something that wouldn't challenge her and make her feel like she didn't belong in her own body.

There was a shout of laughter from the street. Probably some neighborhood kids coming home from a holiday party. Georgette went to the window and looked down at the source of the sound. It looked like someone—Jared? —was riding on someone else's shoulders, swaying wildly as he waved his arms in the air. He snagged something bulky off the fire escape. It fell on him like a heavy blanket, and he overbalanced and half fell off the other man's shoulders. Peals of laughter rang out again.

Georgette turned away from the window. For a moment, she'd imagined James was the other man, but how could that be? He didn't know Jared.

She'd probably never see him again. She didn't *want* to see him again. In fact...

She went over to the stack of paintings against the wall, turning them around to face the room, displaying them side by side by side. James's face staring out at her like a series of fun house mirrors, his dark eyes willing her to believe.

The ghost memory of his fingers trailing along her skin.

No.

This wasn't her life. James. The dreams. The whole thing. She knew who she was, and this wasn't it. Couldn't be. Because it changed everything.

No. It wouldn't change anything. She wouldn't let it.

She grabbed the first painting by the wooden edge of the stretcher and hauled it across the room, ignoring the pull as it seemed to resist her, dragging heavy and slow on the cement floor. She let it fall against the wall by the door and donned her winter coat, then opened the door and gripped the edge of the canvas again. It bumped against each step on the way down, the sound echoing in the stairwell. Finally, she wrangled it outside and down to the Dumpster by the side of the building.

Jared and the other guy were long gone. The street was empty. The wind off the East River sliced through her, shudderingly cold. But she felt good. It was the right thing to do. Closing the door to hauntingly intense James, the random stranger who knew too much about her.

She left the painting leaning against the Dumpster and went inside to get the next one.

The paintings leaned against the Dumpster, out in the cold. One toppled over into the street. A truck ran over it, crunching the edge of the wood frame, crumpling the canvas.

Snow fell onto the canvases, soaked into the painted images. James the stranger, his face obscured, his face melting under the onslaught.

A garbage truck pulled to a stop by the Dumpster. A garbage collector jumped out, grasped a painting with both hands, hauled it up and into the back of the truck. Spinning, grinding blades crushed the wood, the canvas, the paint.

Dream James, memory James, pieces of the past, unknown, unlooked-for, unwanted dreamed of yearned for...

Georgette sat up in bed, tangles of sleepy memories still caught in her brain, vague and inchoate but with an underlying urgent message.

Her winter boots stood by the door. She shoved her bare feet into them, slid her pajama-clad arms into the sleeves of her warm coat, grabbed her copy of Alanna's keys, and bolted downstairs. It was still dark outside. She might be on time. She might be able to rescue the paintings. All that creative outpouring. Whatever it meant, whatever it was, whoever *he* was— it wasn't right to obliterate the best work she'd ever done.

She ran the five blocks to the studio, coat open, the wind rushing through her. Ran like it mattered. One block, two blocks, wait for the light, three blocks. One more to go. A garbage truck lumbered across the street. Heading toward Finn's Fermentation Factory? Or circling back around the one-way street after pulverizing the paintings?

Georgette ran. Passed the truck. Ran faster. Got to the corner.

Across the street, she could see the Dumpster. Beside it, the six paintings.

They were still there.

She could save them.

Back in the studio, back where they belonged, the paintings leaned against the exposed brick wall, all in a row. In her exhausted haze, Georgette imagined they looked worn-out from their adventure.

*Who are you? What did you mean to me?*

*James.*

No. She turned away. She hadn't rescued them because of him. She'd done it because it was her work. Precious hours of creative output. The work mattered. It didn't mean he did.

She shut the door quietly behind her, trying not to picture those dark eyes, that intent gaze, the vividness of his presence.

It wasn't about him.

At all.

Still, as she walked back to Alanna's town house apartment through the dark blue city night, Georgette wondered. Had he found a coat? Was he still out there somewhere, shivering with the cold? Would she dream of him again?

How would she ever paint anything else?

When she got back to Alanna's, she fell onto the sofa bed with her boots on and immediately fell into a deep, dreamless sleep.

Five a.m. Above lazy surf, the sky was inky blue, streaked with the sneaky pale fingers of dawn as if someone had smeared paint randomly across the canvas.

Why did he picture Georgette's long, delicate

fingers covered with light blue and pink paint right now? He'd have to get over that. She was done with him, and anyway, he was here to work.

James picked up his camera again and quickly checked the f-stop and shutter speed. "Ready, guys?"

The ragtag group of middle-aged men shouted back, positively gleeful as they shrugged off their down jackets and sweatpants, revealing spandex bathing suits that clung to their thighs like cut-off wetsuits. "Ready!" "You know it!" "You coming in too, right, Camera Bear?"

He forced himself to grin back at them. The Polar Bear swim was a yearly ritual. It didn't usually make it into the print version of the magazine, but the guys didn't care. They always got a kick out of seeing themselves online.

They raced into the water, gasping as the icy waves lapped their toes. James's camera clicked and clicked, capturing a steady stream of split-second images he'd cull through later. He zoomed in, walked quickly toward the guys, knelt in the sand. Tried to grab the right angles. He was grateful for the distraction, for the need to focus on the here and now.

His eyes felt gritty from lack of sleep and the nightmare images playing at the edges of his mind all night. Georgette at the gorge. Georgette falling. His Georgie, lost to him forever. He'd woken sweaty and shaking, his heart racing and his fists clenched like he was preparing to scramble down the steep slope and try to rescue her all over again.

Here and now was all he had. Press down the shutter, capture laughing men on camera, ignore the rest of the world.

After the shoot, he dove into the Atlantic in his boxers. The guys whooped and hollered from the shore. The cold shock of the ocean water woke up his whole body.

Here and now. Time to let go of the past, finally truly let go.

Georgette drooped into her bowl of Shredded Wheat, half-asleep, her nose practically touching the milky surface.

She shook herself awake, sat up straight, chugged her coffee—which was mostly grounds—and stared down at the list she'd started. She'd put two column headers, like she always did, one for PRO and one for CON.

On the PRO side, she'd written REASONS JAMES IS TELLING THE TRUTH:

On the CON side, she'd written REASONS JAMES IS LYING OR DELUSIONAL:

But that was as far as she'd gotten. Every time she tried to write something, her brain stuttered to a halt, as soggy as the wheat squares in her cereal bowl. Just the word, repeated on the top of the page, JAMES, sent a shiver through her. Last night in the studio felt like a dream, another one in the series. Maybe she should paint it.

Or maybe she should burn the paintings.

Why hadn't she thrown them out?

What did any of it mean?

She picked up her phone and dialed. Her mother. She'd know what this meant. She'd explain it all, couching it in clinical psychological terms Georgette could hold on to. She'd restore sanity.

The phone rang. Once, twice... Georgette was about to disconnect, because how could you leave a message like this? *Mom, I think I may be going crazy, but there's this guy...*

On the third ring, her mother answered.

"Georgette! How lovely to hear from you, and so early!"

"Mom, I'm glad I got you. The weirdest thing happened last night, and—"

"Can we put a pin in it? I'm at Water of Life, about to meet with my meditation instructor. I'll call you later. Oh, and great news. I talked to Dawn. She wants to hire you here in the fall. Isn't that fabulous? They're calling my name, gotta go. Love you."

With that, her mother clicked off.

Fabulous indeed. Water of Life was a spa in the New Mexico desert, set in the vast expanse of red rock and scrubby pines. They believed in a full mind-and-body spiritual awakening, and the on-staff psychologists were an integral part of the experience. It would be a great postdoctoral gig. Perfect, in fact. Another check mark on her five-year plan.

Georgette took her soggy bowl of uneaten cereal to the sink.

"Not eating?" Jared stood in the hallway, rubbing his eyes with his fists. His hair stood up in clumps. He looked as out of it as she felt, which perversely made her feel better.

"Not hungry. What are you doing up?"

"Miles called me. An advertising emergency. Remind me never to become business partners with a guy who thinks the weight of the world rests on his shoulders. Whoops, too late." He gestured to the box of cereal. "If you're done with that…"

Georgette handed it over and poured herself another cup of coffee. Maybe she could inject it straight into her veins, a caffeine IV drip. Surely someone would have invented it by now. She took a sip. Awful stuff. Needed milk and sugar. Lots of sugar. Georgette went back to the dining table.

Jared sat down and started slurping cereal noisily. "So this James."

Georgette nearly dropped her mug. "Excuse me?"

"The guy who climbed the fire escape to see you last night." Jared sauntered over to the dining table with his cereal bowl.

Last night, down in the street. Jared on someone's shoulders. Laughing as he grabbed for something. A bulky fabric sort of something.

James's figure, stark against the window earlier. Coatless.

"You helped him rescue his coat."

Jared sprinkled what looked like half a cup of sugar onto his cereal. "Yup. And then we went out for drinks. Interesting guy." He gave Georgette a sly smile.

"Glad you had a fun evening." She tried to keep an even tone, like it didn't matter. Not one bit. "May I?" She took the sugar bowl and scooped up a spoonful for her coffee.

"Gotta say, I'd never have pegged you for a rebellious teen. My sister, sure. She still is. But you?" Jared's eyes gleamed. He was enjoying this all too much.

She stirred the sugar into her coffee, took a sip. Still too bitter. She would not ask. She would not.

Jared ate a spoonful of cereal. "I hear you haven't been in touch." He cocked his head. "Too bad, I say. He's got way more going on than that drip Sam. Did you know James is a photographer? Extreme sports, he said. He usually shoots for *Adrenaline Rush* magazine. How cool is that? Explains the whole scaling-the-fire-escape thing, no?"

Something peculiar was happening to her insides. Her stomach was turning over, but that could be the sight of Jared slurping his milky cereal. Her chest felt tight, but that could be from sleeping on a sofa-bed mattress. Her head buzzed, though, like unaccustomed thoughts were trying to escape.

She wasn't interested in anything Jared had to say. Wasn't interested in James.

Not even slightly.

She gulped down her coffee and picked up her pencil, determined to write that list. More cons than pros on that list. So many cons. The guy was a con artist who broke into her studio to discombobulate her.

"Don't you want to know what he said about you?"

She gripped her pencil. "No." She glared at Jared. "And please stop talking about that man. I don't care about him."

Jared put his hand up. "Fine!" He got up, bringing his bowl to the sink. "Be that way." He put the bowl in the dishwasher. "You really must have been in love."

The pencil tip broke. "What?"

"Nothing. Never mind. Not saying anything." He

left the room, whistling.

Georgette looked down at her page. The two lists. Rather, the two list headings. So much for lists. She'd drawn an image of a man. In his shirtsleeves. With mussed dark hair, a square jaw, and a perplexed expression.

James.

So much for putting him out of her mind.

# Chapter Five

The girl sat in the therapy office's oversized armchair, feet tucked under her, playing obsessively with the ends of her myriad tiny braids. She looked near tears as she admitted that she felt like a complete failure. Georgette gave an inward sigh of relief. It had taken a long time and a lot of trust-building work for Trudy to open up to her.

Now that she had, the words came out in a torrent. Trudy hated that she was stuck in the family apartment all alone while her parents went to visit her sister's new baby. She felt awful that she'd been grounded yet again. And when Elias, her on-and-off jerk of a boyfriend, texted her drunk photos from a party he hadn't invited her to, she'd gone to the medicine cabinet and grabbed a huge handful of her mom's Xanax. She'd made herself throw up before they hit her stomach, but what about next time?

Georgette wanted to hug her, wanted to tell her to be strong, that she'd grow up and become her own woman, that her parents were clueless morons. But that wasn't how this worked. So she handed over the Kleenex box and guided her client closer to independence and self-confidence.

Trudy blew her nose. "I'm a mess, huh?"

"Life is messy. You're doing great. Confronting the pain is hard. You're braver than most girls your age."

Trudy tossed the tissue into the trash and handed the box back. "You look like you can use them more than me." She indicated Georgette's lap.

Oh. She'd apparently been taking tissues out of the box all session and tearing them into tiny bits.

Georgette gathered the bits and squeezed them, as if she could make them regenerate into a whole sheet once more. "Just the way I listen. I fiddle."

"Never seen you do it before, Doc."

Georgette gave her a rueful smile. "You're an observant person. You'll go far." Whenever possible, turn the subject back to the patient's needs.

Trudy, with her tight cornrows close to her scalp and her midriff shirts that bared her deep brown belly even in winter, wasn't exactly a mirror for Georgette as a teenager. And yet she felt a kinship with the girl.

At the end of the session, she gave Trudy her cell phone number and made her promise to call if she started to drown. The past hour had been a breakthrough for tough-tender Trudy. This was why she'd trained to be a psychologist. Helping someone heal. It felt so right, it almost hurt.

After Trudy left, Georgette picked up the scraps of tissue that had gotten caught in the rug. It was true. She wasn't a fidgety person. Not usually. But today, she

felt like she'd been caught in a snowstorm, except that
the blizzard was inside her head, making it hard to
think straight. And this—she opened her hand and let
the bits drift back down to the floor like a gentle
snowfall—it was the external manifestation.

She needed to pull herself together. As she walked
out of the building into the winter chill, she pulled her
phone out of her bag.

Her mother picked up on the first ring. "Now I
know something's up. Two calls in the space of a
morning? What's going on? Holiday blues? Second
thoughts about staying in the city for the break? I still
think it best, but if you…"

"Do you remember a boy named James? From
Pine Mountain? A…friend of mine?" *Tell me what this
means. Tell me I haven't forgotten a huge chunk of my
past.*

The scent of a pretzel vendor's wares wafted into
the air, making her stomach turn over.

Her mother was quiet for a too-long beat. "It was
a long time ago. I can't say I remember all your
friends." But her silence had given her away.

"Tallish, dark hair. He—" She faltered. What else
did she know about him? She walked faster, her heels
clicking on the cement in a rat-tat-tat rhythm.

*The time my dad busted us for loitering under the
bridge.*

"I think his dad was a cop. I think... I think maybe James was important to me."

"Georgette, are you okay? You don't sound like yourself."

"I'm fine." She forced herself to walk slower, talk slower, take breaths. "I'm starting to feel like I might not remember everything from that part of my life. Before the accident. Is that possible?"

"None of us remember everything. That's how memory works, pruning away the inessentials."

"What if something isn't inessential?"

"Then you remember it." Her mother's matter-of-fact tone made it sound so simple.

"But the accident itself... I can't remember..."

"Physical trauma will do that. You probably blacked out right away. But you survived. That's the important thing." Her mother's shaky voice belied her psychologist language.

By now, Georgette had reached the subway station. She paused by the green entrance poles, not ready to go down the steps and risk losing the signal.

"I'm sure you're right, but—"

Her mother interrupted. "Wait, now I recall that James boy. He wasn't your type. Rough around the edges. Not a great student. But he kept showing up on our doorstep with wildflowers. Daisies and forget-me-nots he'd no doubt plucked by the side of the road.

Wrapped in a McDonald's fries wrapper, of all things. And then, when you wouldn't come to the door, he'd stomp off and ride away on his motorcycle." She said it disdainfully. "Not your type at all."

Her mother made him sound like a teenage stalker. "Did I ever go out with him?"

"Once or twice. That's why you don't remember. He wasn't important to your personal growth. Not like Brian. Have you heard from him lately?"

Brian was her first college boyfriend. Her parents had fallen all over him like he was going to be Georgette's savior, supplying them with a steady stream of grandchildren and funny anecdotes. He was witty, she'd give him that. But she'd broken up with him after freshman year. She'd heard his stories too many times, and it turned out there wasn't much more to him than that. "I think he's in LA, finishing up his plastic surgery residency."

"Good for him. So, was that why you called? High school reminiscences? Very common this time of year. Everyone's in nostalgia mode. Honey, if you miss being home for the break, we can reconsider."

"No, I'm fine here. It's just…" She took a breath. They didn't talk about this. The subject was taboo. "The accident. I was alone, right?"

She'd gone swimming, her parents told her. At the reservoir outside Pine Mountain, the small Adirondack town where they'd lived her first few years of high school. You ducked through the hole in the wire-link fence, pushed your way through trees and overgrown brush, and scrambled down a treacherously steep cliff to the inviting pool below.

But she didn't remember diving. Didn't remember the moment of impact. Didn't remember that trip to the swimming hole at all. It was as if the entire day had been erased by her head injury.

"We've gone over this." Her mother's voice was gentle. "Remember our mantra?"

Georgette took a calming breath, then another. The way her mother had taught her. Long, slow breaths counteracted panic, sent oxygen to the brain, allowed you to regain your equilibrium. "Past is done. Move forward, one careful step at a time."

"It sounds like you're spiraling, honey. You need to be careful."

"I know." All too well.

It had taken two weeks for her to regain consciousness after the accident. Two months to recognize familiar faces. Four months to pick up a fork and knife without dropping them. A year to walk without a cane.

Every time she threw her spoon across the room in frustration or bowed her head over the crutches in utter exhaustion, her mother would come over, rub her

shoulders, and have her repeat the mantra. *Past is done.*
*Move forward, one careful step at a time.* Sometimes
she'd add, "And you're not going to take that kind of
risk again, right?" And Georgette would agree. She
wouldn't. Not ever.

Now her mother said, "You mean the world to me
and your father, you know that, right?"

And she did.

This close to winter break, the hallways of the
University of New York echoed with the silence of a
thousand absent undergrads. But Georgette's mentor,
Professor Adele Kinsella, was ensconced in her cozy
office as usual, surrounded by piles of printouts,
psychology journals, and scribbled notes in her
trademark hasty scrawl.

Georgette put the folder down on Professor
Kinsella's desk and patted it fondly. "Everything from
my sessions with Trudy to date. Nothing new, you've
heard it all in our debriefings, but it's in one place now,
for my end-of-semester report."

The professor regarded her over frameless reading
glasses. "You like her, don't you?"

"I like working with her. She's honest."

"Teens often are. You have to know how to listen
to them so they don't shut you out. They're shaping
their future selves. It's a delicate time."

What if their future selves didn't remember? "Professor. I, uh…" She stuttered to a stop.

This got the older woman's attention. She raised one eyebrow. Georgette never stumbled over her words, but this time… Well. This time.

"I was wondering how much you know about selective amnesia and the long-term effects."

"One of your patients? None of them presented with anything like that. Did it come up in a session?"

"Not a patient, no. Is it possible to forget a profoundly important part of your life but remember other things—and other people—from the same basic time frame?"

The professor tapped her pen against the desk. "Amnesia in any form is fairly rare, but selective amnesia…" She shook her head. "It's rather fascinating, isn't it? First you need to determine whether it's psychogenic or caused by trauma to the head."

She'd always assumed she'd lost the immediate events of that afternoon, but no more than that. Could the accident have erased her memories of James? Of an entire relationship? Was that even possible?

"Do you know how long ago the amnesia began? Is it isolated to a specific time frame?"

Georgette snapped back to the conversation. "Ten years. And yes, I believe so."

"Are you talking about someone you know personally, or something you read?"

"Someone I know." She felt telltale heat rise in her cheeks.

Her mentor took off her reading glasses and folded them with small, precise movements. "This isn't a friend, is it?" She addressed the glasses, not Georgette. "It's you."

"I…" But the words were stuck. They wouldn't come. It felt as if speaking would make it all true. "I don't know. Maybe." That felt safer.

"Sit." The older woman gestured to the chair across from her.

Georgette sat. She set her shoulder bag on her lap, needing the reassuring weight. "It might not be anything. I mean…" What did she mean?

"I understand. It might be uncomfortable to confront this. Well, of course it is, or else you wouldn't have blocked the memories."

"If that's what they are."

"Explain."

So Georgette told her. The dreams, the paintings, James appearing in her window. What her mother said. The accident.

Professor Kinsella was a wonderful listener. Nodding, *hmm*ing, her eyes warm and her expression softly inviting.

Finally, Georgette sat back, surprised to find her arms quivering with tension. "Like my mother said, James must not have meant much to me, or I'd have remembered him." She laced her fingers together, keeping them steady.

Professor Kinsella pursed her mouth. "You're an excellent clinician. If a patient told you these same details—including the fact that the patient had stopped attending therapy sessions when the dreams emerged..." Her gaze was stern now, and Georgette ducked her head. But she continued without an explicit scold, "How would you analyze the situation?"

Georgette closed her eyes, trying to picture it. Trudy, maybe, or one of her other patients, saying she'd dreamed about a man and then he'd shown up. "He must have been important to me. My subconscious has been all but breaking down the door, shouting at me to let the memories back in."

"That sounds about right. I fear if you don't open yourself up to the memories, you'll have other problems. Psychosomatic ailments, a depression/fear cycle, or some other manifestation of suppressed turmoil. Things like this are best brought into the light of day."

Georgette heaved a sigh. "But how?"

"Find a memory trigger. Hypnosis, if necessary. Seeing this James again. Possibly returning to the site of the accident."

Her head throbbed, a sudden, sharp pain. She rubbed the spot, feeling the ridges under her fingers—old scar tissue. "It feels overwhelming."

"I can imagine. Be gentle with yourself. Something like this is likely to shake up your entire sense of identity. Part of your past is missing, and that part might well have shaped you into a different person. Uncovering it means figuring out how to fold it into who you've become since then. You may feel fragmented for a while. It's likely to be a scary place to dwell. But worth it, in the end." Dr. Kinsella gave Georgette a gentle, compassionate smile. "And it will make you a phenomenal psychologist. You'll have true insight into the nature of personality, the kind of thing the rest of us grope in the dark searching for."

Georgette's head was pounding, the pain beating in rhythm with her heart. She stood. "Thank you, Professor. You've given me a lot to think about."

# Chapter Six

The *Adrenaline Rush* magazine office, it turned out, was around the corner from the café where she'd first seen James from the bus window. Two blocks from the apartment she'd shared with Sam.

Which meant she'd walked past this corner, this street, countless times. Had James ever been walking in the opposite direction? Maybe he'd been busy on his phone and she'd been focused on her pastry. Neither of them looking up, neither noticing the other.

Now Georgette stood, hyperaware, focused on the narrow brick building across the street that housed the magazine office. A flower shop took up the storefront space.

The wind bit her cheeks and the edges of her ears. She wrapped her scarf tighter around her neck. The streetscape was filled with people. None of them was James.

A man emerged from the shop holding a bouquet of orchids. He was tall, with messy dark hair and strong shoulders, wearing a dark jacket. Georgette's pulse quickened, but it wasn't him.

The bitter wind sliced through her, colder by the second. This was a fool's errand. If she wanted to see James, she should go into the office and ask for him. If he wasn't there, she could get his phone number—or at least his last name.

She should.

She would.

In another minute. Or five. Or ten.

Or never.

Because going in and asking for him, seeking him out, that risked *him* seeing *her*. She'd be confronted by that dark, piercing gaze that turned her inside out. As if he held the keys to her innermost self. The thought made her shiver, and it wasn't just the bitingly cold air.

She turned back toward the bus stop, ready to give up, more than a little relieved. Maybe it was just as well if she didn't see him. Given enough time, the dreams would fade away on their own. This was more than a fool's errand, it was a misguided one. Past was done.

The door to the building swung open. Two people stepped outside. A slender light-skinned black woman with a beautifully tailored coat and scarf—and a man. Tall, with dark, unruly hair, wearing a brown leather bomber jacket and a thick wool scarf, holding a paper cup with tendrils of steam rising from the top. A man who wore his jeans like a second skin, with an uncanny ease in his body, the ease of someone who knew who he was, who lived outdoors. A man she knew like a second heartbeat.

They paused after they got outside. The woman put her hand on James's arm. Georgette's chest tightened. Who was this woman to him? A lover? Her body language said she wanted to be. His said he was thinking about it. Letting her lean in toward him. Listening, nodding thoughtfully.

Without thinking, Georgette moved forward, oblivious to her own surroundings.

"Hey!" A white-haired man plowed into her, his grocery bags spilling out of his arms.

"Oh God, I'm so sorry!" She knelt to help him gather the groceries.

He made a harrumphing noise. "Tourist."

"I was preoccupied. I *am* sorry." She put a can of chickpeas into the shopping bag.

He humphed again, sounding slightly mollified.

Someone else knelt to help.

Georgette's skin prickled with his nearness. He smelled of familiarity and foreignness, woodlands and secrets. Even before she consciously processed the signifiers, she knew. "James."

He picked up a box of rice. "Georgette." His voice rumbled through her. "This *is* a surprise."

When James spotted Georgette kneeling on the sidewalk, he'd have thought he was hallucinating her—except that he'd have imagined her standing on a street corner with the wind ruffling her dark waves of hair, staring longingly at him. Not on her knees, surrounded by a tumble of groceries.

He said a hasty good-bye to Maggie and crossed the street to rescue Georgette.

After the groceries were reassembled and their owner sent on his way, Georgette put her hand on James's sleeve. The look in her eyes, the tilt of her head —it shot through him, a visceral response. His Georgette was back. She looked more vibrant than she had last night. More alive. More like the girl he remembered. Like she'd woken up. "Thank you for helping me out. I think it would be good if we talked, now that I'm over the shock of last night. Can we?"

Her meltingly familiar contralto combined with her hand on his sleeve, that tentative touch—it ripped him open.

He was sixteen and Georgette was shouting to him across the school cafeteria in mid-September, and the way she called his name sent goose bumps down his spine, because he knew. They were going to be together.

He was seventeen, and so was she, in a quiet playground at night. It was warm for November but still chilly. They'd snuck away from a friend's party to have some privacy. They were entangled, sharing a wide swing, kissing frantically. She whispered his name against his mouth, and he desperately wanted more, wanted to do everything with her, but simultaneously wanted to hold on to the moment forever, just kissing. Anticipating, building, ready, but not quite there yet. Forever on the verge of discovery.

He was celebrating his seventeenth birthday with Georgette in his parents' basement in late spring and she was talking into the phone, telling her parents that yes, she was with him and she planned to spend the entire evening there whether they liked it or not. Her voice was firm, but with a tremble under the surface. Like now. And he knew. She was going to break up with him.

It was Labor Day weekend, and she stood at the top of the gorge, the wind playing with her sundress, the reservoir a hideously long way down. She'd given him a hot, angry look, and...

"James." Her voice brought him back to the present. "It's cold out here. Can we?" She gestured to the deli.

Something was different in her posture—a hesitant vulnerability. Last night, she'd folded her arms across her chest, held her paintbrush like a weapon. Today she seemed open. Almost yearning.

His breath caught. "Did you remember me? Us? Is that why you want to talk?"

The air between them vibrated. She gazed at him

like she was going to reveal something intimate and important. Then she looked away, clearly thinking better of it. "No. It's just that it was a lot to digest. Imagine you discovered that you didn't remember someone. Someone who had apparently been important to you. That the memory wasn't there."

His chest felt tight. The familiar jittery restlessness was back. He covered with a light tone. "So how can I help you?" He quirked an eyebrow and was rewarded with a tentative smile in return, the first he'd seen from her.

She let out her breath in a whoosh, the steam lingering in the chilled air. "I spoke with my mother today. She said..." She gathered herself up. Standing straight, no longer touching his sleeve. "She said you and I went on a couple of dates, if that. That you were hot for me, but I wasn't... Well."

"And you believed her?" James flipped up the top of his coffee cup, mostly to have something to do that didn't involve looking at Georgette.

"Why would she lie?" Another breath coalesced in the space between them, then dissipated.

"I can think of a lot of reasons." *Too many.* "If you believe her, I don't see what we have to talk about."

Still Georgette hesitated.

"So you don't believe her?" Hope opened up space in his chest.

"How can I know? I don't remember!" She ran impatient hands through her hair, tugged on the ends. "It feels like the memory is just out of reach. Like the feeling when you can't think of a word, but you can feel its shape on your tongue. Only this is an entire chunk of my life." She shook her head like she was trying to dislodge the memories by force.

He wanted to smooth her hair back into place. Instead, he took a sip of coffee, then winced. Too hot. Now his tongue was seared, and his heart—well. "I don't have any magic pill to make you remember me, sorry. Have you made one of your lists yet? *Things I Remember* or *What James Said to Me*."

Her eyes widened. "You know about the lists?"

He grinned despite himself. "You *do* still make them, then."

"I—maybe." A dimple peeked out of her cheek, then quickly disappeared. That dimple. Adorable as ever, dammit. But then she seemed to close up, become more formal. "That's not relevant. Can we go somewhere to talk?"

"For a minute. I have to get back in there." He gestured across the street toward the magazine offices. "I stepped out to clear my head." Of thoughts of her. The irony was infinitely amusing.

"How about the Stone Cold Café? That's the place where..." She faltered. "Where I saw you from the bus."

He fell into step alongside her. But as they rounded the corner toward the café, a man barreled into them, seemingly on purpose, his gaze fixed on Georgette. "Georgie!" His tone was aggressive.

James stepped in front of Georgette, feeling a sudden surge of protectiveness. "Watch it."

The guy—dark skin, indeterminate race, tall and geeky—switched his gaze to James. Looking aghast, he stumbled back. "Oh my God."

If he was going to have this effect on all New Yorkers, it might be time to head back home to Pine Mountain.

But Georgette stepped out from behind James. "Sam, it's not like that."

*Like what?*

The guy recovered his equilibrium. "Goddamn it, you *do* exist! I knew it!"

James blinked. He *existed?*

"You told me you dreamed him up. You told me he wasn't real, the paintings were from your imagination. Some imagination." He gave James a poisonous look. "Enjoy her while you have her. Before she cheats on you too."

Georgette reached out to Sam, gripping his shoulder. "I never cheated on you. Not with him, not with anyone."

"Yeah. Whatever." The guy wrenched himself away from her and stomped down the sidewalk.

Georgette stared after him, shaking her head. "Oh, Sam." She turned to James. "I'm so sorry. I have to talk to him. I can't leave him in this state. He's too fragile."

A shot of jealousy coursed through him, leaving a sour aftertaste and a jittery restlessness. But what else could he say? "Of course. Go." And then he watched her thread her way through the afternoon crowd to her ex-boyfriend, who didn't seem at all pleased to see her.

It wasn't until an hour later, when he was back in front of his borrowed office computer, deep in Photoshop hell, that James realized he hadn't gotten her phone number. Again. And hadn't given her his.

And her ex's words rang in his head on an endless loop.

*"You told me you dreamed him up. You told me he wasn't real, the paintings were from your imagination."*

What the hell had he meant?

"You gonna have your own rig setup so you can jump alongside us?" Blake, the lead glider with his close-cropped hair, his dark Aborigine skin, and his thick Australian accent, peered out of the laptop screen at James.

"What do you think?" James forced himself to put a smile into his voice, or Blake and his crew would think something was wrong with their plans. "I wouldn't miss it."

"Adrenaline junkie."

"Takes one to know one."

Blake's face split into a grin. "It's going to be amazing. Springtime in the city, the trees in full bloom, those skyscrapers behind us and between us, and us swooping like seagulls." He made a diving motion with his cupped hands. "A*maz*ing."

"Does this mean you got the permits? The city's approved?"

Blake waved his hand airily. "They'll come through. No worries, mate." He leaned forward. "We'll come in a week ahead as planned. Got the tickets lined up yesterday. Wingsuits go on ahead in cargo. You'll scout the location and send shots to us, yeah?"

They'd climbed the bank tower in Jersey City last summer when Blake came through to do a miles-long glide along the Delaware River, but it was hypothetical back then. Now it was real. James felt the frisson of excitement in his gut that said, *Yes, this. This is why I do what I do.* Diving, soaring, skimming the ground at ridiculously high speeds, heart pounding in his chest. Cheating death.

And with the thought came an image of Georgette, but not the woman he'd met this week. The girl he'd known ten years ago. The one who had learned who she was with him. The one who threw her arms wide on his motorcycle and laughed when the wind snatched her barrette away, letting her hair blow crazily around her head. He'd shouted at her to put her helmet on, but she'd just laughed harder.

*"Goddamn it, you do exist! I knew it!"* What the hell did that mean? What paintings?

"Mate? You okay? This project too much for you?" Blake frowned at him through the screen.

"Hell no, looking forward to it. But you have to send me the permits ahead of time. You know how Maggie gets. The magazine won't run the piece if you haven't gotten the right official papers filed with the state."

"Yeah, yeah. No worries, *Mom*." Blake laughed and disconnected from Skype.

James closed his computer and stood up, then paced to the window. He leaned on the radiator, looking out over a sliver of Midtown, lit up for nighttime like an overdecorated Christmas tree, decked out with neon and flashing video screens. It made him seasick.

He had to get out of this tiny hotel room.

He grabbed his jacket and left, shoving his wallet and phone into his pants.

# Chapter Seven

Last night, the place had been nearly deserted except for the lit windows on the third floor. Tonight, though, the third floor was dark, while four men incongruously dressed in elegant jackets were loading up a truck on the ground floor with boxes.

James hesitated. He should ask these guys if he could go up to the third floor. That was the straightforward thing to do. But what if they said no? Or didn't have the studio key? The men clearly worked at Finn's Fermentation Factory. The air around them was permeated with brine and vinegar.

He slipped around the corner to the side of the building and gazed up at the fire escape. This time he wouldn't let his jacket get caught. He took it off, folded it neatly on the sidewalk, then took a running leap at the wall. The sound of a truck engine firing gave him an extra burst of energy, and he snagged the iron edge of the landing on his first try. Swinging from one hand, he hoisted himself up. Success!

"What the hell do you think you're doing?"

James peered down. A sandy-haired man with a smock over his dark silk shirt stared up from the sidewalk. Behind him, the truck drove away down the quiet street.

"I wanted to see the view from the top."

"Very funny. You need to come down now."

James dropped back down to the sidewalk. It had been such a perfect moment too, latching on to the fire escape his first try.

He wiped his hands on his pants, then thrust out his right hand. "James Falk. I'm assuming you're Finn? Or is it Mr. Finn?"

"It's Mr. McKenna to you." Finn gave him a dark look.

"Sorry. I should have asked before climbing up. But I did it last night, so I thought…"

"Excuse me?" The man's tone got even sharper.

"I was visiting Georgette Soren. Do you know her?"

"I rent the space to her and her friends. You climbed the fire escape to visit her?" If anything, Finn seemed more bristly at this revelation, not less.

"Maybe I should explain."

"Maybe you should go back to Nassau Avenue and forget this whole thing." Finn raked his hands through his hair. He smelled pleasantly of dill and basil.

"I'm in love with her." It came out abruptly. Startlingly. And not as far from true as he'd have liked. "And I think she might be painting me. I had to see for myself. I mean, painting me, that means something, right?" James gestured up at the fire escape.

"I didn't think you'd let me in if I asked, so…"

"You thought right." But Finn looked marginally warmer.

James picked up his leather jacket and donned it. "I don't suppose you'd consider letting me in? You can stick around."

Finn folded his arms. "You're in love with her?"

"High school sweethearts. We ran into each other recently. There's still chemistry." He mentally crossed his fingers behind his back. Everything he said was technically true.

"What about Sam? They're barely broken up, and you're trying to horn in?"

James snorted. "That poser with the sad eyes and the ridiculous scarf? Sure seems over him to me."

Finn laughed. "There's that." He regarded James for another moment, then gave a brusque nod and started heading toward the corner. "Come on, then. But make it quick. I'm due at a party. My wife is probably already wondering where I am."

The studio was a study in shadows. Large paintings loomed along one wall, their scary subjects half-visible in the dark, mere hints of gleaming eyes and sharp fangs. Monsters from the id.

A series of smaller paintings leaned against another wall, a set of images of a dark-haired man with a runner's physique, done in varying styles.

James glanced over at McKenna, who stood by the door looking impatient, then turned to the final wall of artwork hidden behind a group of shrouded sculptures. This set of canvases was turned toward the wall, as if the paintings were feeling shy.

With an icy tingle of premonition, he turned the first canvas around.

It was him.

Georgette wasn't quite as polished an artist as her friend. Her work was more raw, less refined. And the likeness wasn't exact. The face was wider, and the hair

—

But it was recognizably him as a teenager. His tormented face filled the canvas.

Afraid to find out what was next, he turned the second canvas around.

Him again. Crouching in an empty room, hands in his hair.

Were they all like this? What about the fun times? What about laughing together, snowball fights, exhilarating bicycle chases, in-jokes, and long make-out sessions in the tall grass?

He turned the third canvas around and stepped back in shock.

Him again, but at twenty-seven, not seventeen. Now, not then. Sitting on a bench on a subway platform. Clad in the bomber jacket he wore now. He touched his sleeve to check. Yes. This one.

He gingerly touched the canvas with his forefinger. The paint was dry. She'd painted this a while ago.

He stepped back. Spooked.

Behind him, Finn whistled. He'd come closer while James was staring at the multiplicity of painted reflections. "You weren't kidding. They're all you." He gave James a measuring look. "You don't seem happy about it."

James rubbed his face, feeling the sandpaper scrape of incipient stubble. "I need to talk to her. Not that it's going to happen."

"Why not?"

"I don't know how to reach her. I don't even know where she lives." He turned away. "Thanks for letting me in. I appreciate it. You should probably get to your party."

Finn flicked off the light closest to the paintings. "Come with me."

"What?"

"Georgette will be there. You can talk to her." He started walking, apparently assuming James would follow.

Feeling like he'd stepped into a parallel universe, James followed his new friend out the door and down the stairs.

The party was in a three-story glass-walled office building on the Dumbo waterfront, the arches of the Manhattan and Brooklyn Bridges visible beyond it. Bouncers stood outside, checking names. Lights from inside flashed multicolored arcs onto the sidewalk. Partygoers were dressed to stun, if not kill.

Georgette's steps slowed as she took in the sight. Next to her, Hayley stopped dead in her tracks. "*That's* the party? I don't think so."

Alanna put her hand on her boyfriend Miles's arm, halting their progress, and twisted around to face her friends. "Afraid one of your old Occupy buddies might see you going in and think less of you?"

Hayley snorted. "I'm afraid I'll say something to the wrong person and get punched in the nose. I think I'll head over to Suzu's for a rousing game of Scrabble."

Their fourth studio mate, Susannah, had cancelled on them at the last minute, saying she was coming down with a cold. She didn't like crowds. Or, really, people. Hayley simply didn't like rich people.

Georgette poked her. "Come on, we can make fun of the one percent together. How can you properly fight them if you haven't seen them up close?"

"Fine. But don't make me stay."

"Long enough to make fun of the decor, taste Finn's new concoctions, and give Raven a hug. We'll head back to Greenpoint together."

"Promise?"

"Pinky swear." Georgette held out her hand, pinky cocked.

Alanna gave Georgette a wink and linked her arm through Miles's, continuing on to join the long line.

The party was loud, dark, and insanely crowded. James had been hunting for Georgette for half an hour with no luck.

It was a wild space. If the *Times* and *Architectural Digest* hadn't both done multipage spreads on the building's design, the developers should fire their PR firm. Desks in playful hues sprang from the floor at different heights, huge glass flowers covered the ceiling, and there was a slide in the center of the room, a dark swirl of a tube heading down to the second floor.

A cater waiter stood patiently by the opening, taking plates and long-stemmed glasses from each party guest before they plunged down the chute. Shrieks emanated from the tube.

James threaded through the immense crowd and approached the chute as two women handed over their plates to the waiter, ready to go down the slide.

One was Georgette.

Even Hayley admitted it would be cool to go

down a translucent slide between floors in a glass office building, but only if Georgette came with her. It took several minutes to get to the front of the line, most of which Hayley spent staring daggers at Luka Vuković, the hotshot young playboy developer who'd helped design this place and was currently giving an interview to a local news station.

Hayley whispered loudly that he was an overentitled devil in a Hugo Boss suit, and if this line didn't move any faster, she was going to march over and tell him how she felt about his family's Disneyfication of the Long Island City waterfront.

Georgette was grateful to get to the front of the line. When Hayley got like this, there was no telling what she might do. At least this way, they'd have a floor between them and Vuković.

She yanked down her skirt, preparing to sit and slide.

And then she heard someone call her name. A jolt of awareness shot through her.

James. Here. As he shouldered his way through the crowd, she had that strange feeling again, like he held some kind of key. Like he *knew* her. She shivered, but this time it wasn't with cold. It was all him.

The skinny, overdressed guy behind her frowned. "You're holding up the line."

"Come on!" Hayley tugged her hand.

She took a small step toward James as he came up, intending to leave the line and see what he had to say. His gaze burned through her. But it was so crowded. Someone bumped James, he crashed into her, and Hayley hastily jumped back to avoid falling.

James grabbed Georgette's shoulders to steady her. She took an inadvertent step toward him, compelled by his closeness.

The guy in charge of the slide frowned at them. "Someone's gotta go down. Now."

Hayley crouched. "I'm going. Don't be long." She took off with a whoop that echoed back up the tunnel.

Then it was Georgette's turn. She glanced at James. "I'll wait for you on the second floor. We'll talk there." She knelt at the edge of the tube. The tube loomed ahead, dark and swirling and endless. Her stomach clenched. She gripped the nearest surface and felt hard muscle under soft cotton. James's shirt. James's arm. But she couldn't stop looking into the abyss.

"You don't have to go down." James's soft voice penetrated her paralysis.

"I do, though." She wasn't about to let a stupid Plexiglas tube defeat her. "It's just a slide." *Not a cliff. Not a steep drop onto rocks and water. Not a catastrophe.*

She might not remember, but her body did.

She grabbed on to James for support, clutching his shirt sleeve. He slid in behind her, nestling her against him. "Want to do this?" His breath tickled her ear. His soft voice penetrated her fear. She assented. It was the only way.

They slid down, jostling against each other in the narrow confines of the tunnel. As the crush of partygoers, the brightly lit bridges outside, and the darkly colorful rooms flashed by in a dizzying swirl, Georgette felt James against her like a warm wall, steadying and sure, and her panic subsided.

And she remembered.

*Snow tubing, riding belly-down in a car tire down a twisty snowy slope, laughing, careening wildly, falling off, rolling into James's arms. Kissing.*

*Sledding across slick fresh snow, tree branches whipping past as she'd leaned back against his hard chest and wished the hill would go on forever.*

They popped out of the chute on the ground floor and staggered to stand. Her footing felt unsteady and unsure. James was right beside her, gazing down with concern. She gave him a wobbly smile. She'd survived the dreaded children's slide.

Oblivious, Hayley put her hand up for a high five. "Wasn't that awesome? Even the devil gets things right sometimes." She checked James out. "Who are you, anyway?" She gave Georgette a reproving look. "You didn't tell me you had a new guy."

Georgette squirmed. "I knew James in high

school." And with that, her euphoria was gone, popped like so many soap bubbles.

"So you admit it," he said softly. He didn't seem victorious. Anything but. His next words revealed why. "I saw the paintings. We need to talk."

Georgette's mind went blank. "You went to the studio?"

Hayley gazed between the two of them. "*That's* where I saw you before. Those paintings. That's you?"

"So it seems." His gaze sliced into Georgette, sharp and painful. "Why did you lie to me? You claim not to remember, but those paintings, they say you did all along."

Georgette glanced at Hayley, who was eagerly, blatantly eavesdropping. The music thudded in her ears, and behind them, someone emerged from the tube with a whoosh and a happy yell. "Can we go somewhere private?"

# Chapter Eight

When Georgette pulled him past the heavy door and into the back stairwell, James could feel her hand trembling.

On his way over in the truck with Finn, he hadn't been able to get the image of her in the studio out of his brain, acting shocked to see him. Had she lied to him to mess with his mind? He'd gritted his teeth so hard, his jaw still hurt.

But then the way Georgette had paused, frozen with fear at the mouth of the slide, obviously reliving her traumatic fall into the gorge, and the way her hand trembled now—it changed everything.

Whatever she knew or didn't know, she was clearly not lying to torment him. So what the hell was the meaning of those paintings?

As soon as the hallway door closed with a hushed click behind them, he let go of her hand and spun her around to face him. "Explain."

Georgette crossed her arms, looking strangely fragile. "You saw the paintings. It seems like I must remember you, right?"

"You think?"

"But I don't. Except that I started dreaming about you about six months ago."

"Dreaming?"

"Not those sorts of dreams." But she didn't meet his gaze, and her breath stuttered. She ran her hand along the curve of banister on the stair landing, an unconsciously sensual caress.

His body responded with a startlingly powerful surge of lust. *Down, boy. Not now.*

"The paintings, they're from the dreams?"

She nodded.

Those paintings, the ones of him crouched in an empty room. Him alone on the subway platform.

His lust drained away. "Why did you paint me? If you didn't know who I was."

"I couldn't get you out of my head. The dreams were so haunting." She met his gaze. Their connection flared, startling in its power. "I thought you were a manifestation of an unexplored need to assert my masculine side."

He blinked. "Your what?"

She gave him a crooked smile. "I'm getting my PhD in psychology. I can't help it, that's how I think. And I thought…" She hesitated. Her hair was falling out of her braid, there was a pucker between her eyebrows, and her cheeks were pink with embarrassment. Awareness sent a prickle down his spine. This was altogether too intimate. This was making him want to kiss her, push her up against the wall...

*Deep breath. Stay focused. Don't look at her lips. Don't remember what it felt like to have her in your arms.*

"You thought..."

"You were so intense in my dreams. So passionate." Her flush grew deeper. "I thought it was my subconscious telling me I needed to find more passion in my life."

*Oh God.*

"When I saw you through the bus window, I thought I was hallucinating." Her voice dropped to a whisper. "But I wasn't."

"You weren't." They were inches apart. The air between them felt charged, electric. A much-needed cooling breeze slid through him from above. Someone must have left the roof door open.

Georgette shook her head as if coming out of a trance. "So that's it. It's simple, when you come down to it."

"Simple." The breeze shivered on his skin. She'd been dreaming about him for six months. Dreams that meant so much, she felt compelled to paint them.

Everything he'd wanted. Except also not. She hadn't known who he was.

After the accident, when she was still in a coma, he'd gone to the hospital. Raced up seven flights of stairs instead of waiting for the pokey elevator. The last time he'd seen her, the paramedics were gently extricating her unresponsive hand from his panicked grip so they could load her stretcher onto the waiting copter. "She'll be okay," a plump, balding paramedic had said, but his kind eyes said it was a lie.

It couldn't be a lie. He had to see her. See for himself that she'd survived. She was in a coma, his mother said, but that didn't mean anything, did it? She'd respond to him, she'd wake up and smile and he'd be the hero who'd brought his sleeping beauty back to life.

But the doors to the ICU wing were closed, and a security guard refused to let him through. "Immediate family only." But James couldn't leave. Georgette was in there, in a sterile room, tubes attached to her body. He needed to hold her hand, stroke her forehead. Be there.

When her father strode through, looking haggard, James rushed up to him. "Mr. Soren, how is she? Can I see her? If you tell him…" He gestured to the guard.

But the older man shook him off like he was a mosquito. Worse, because it wasn't disdain in his posture, it was fear. "Get out of here. Haven't you done enough damage? I don't want to see you here again." And he brushed past and into the hushed hospital wing.

James never saw her again. When he went to

Albuquerque, driving his fifteen-year-old truck across the whole damned country to see his Georgette, she hadn't even come to the door.

He'd kept going that time. Driven the breadth of the country, down to Texas and up to Washington State. Gotten a passport and driven that old clinker up to Alaska. Deferred college and driven down through Mexico. Kept going. Moving felt better than sitting. Action better than thought.

That familiar itchy restlessness was back. He had to move. Wanted to grab her. Wanted to run, climb, *go.*

Cool air. The roof. An open door, an implicit invitation.

He headed for the steps going up.

"James?" Georgette stood below him on the landing, gripping the banister, puzzled.

He gestured up the stairs, toward the top. "I can't stay in here. The air, it's stale. I can't breathe."

One minute, it seemed like James was about to crush her against his long body and kiss her—and the next, he echoed her "Simple," and then headed up to the roof, taking the steps two at a time.

Spending time with this man was an exercise in expecting the unexpected.

James paused on the stairs. His eyes gleamed.

"Come on."

"Where?"

"Don't you want a little adventure? Don't you ever want to break out of your safe life?"

"But…are we done talking?"

"We can talk on the roof."

So she went up too. The muffled sounds of the ongoing party felt miles away as James pushed open the door to the outside world. He held it open for her, gesturing with an elegant sweep of his hand. "After you, my lady."

She stepped out onto the flat roof. The air was cool against the bare skin of her throat. It felt refreshing. Like waking up.

James strode past groupings of brightly painted metal chairs and huge empty planters, heading straight to the edge. He looked back at her, his gaze teasing. "Coming?" Beyond him, the lights of Manhattan skyscrapers shone like a movie backdrop.

The cool breeze ruffled his dark hair. His movements were so sure, his stride so eager. He looked more alive than she'd seen him. Lit from within.

She went.

He stood by the edge, taking shots of the view with a small camera he'd fished out of his pocket.

The Manhattan skyline, the dark rippling water of the East River, the twin bridge spans edged with lights, the multicolored lights streaming from the party below them, the crowd lined up across the street even at this hour to sample Grimaldi's pizza, and the man next to her, vibratingly present—it was all kind of perfect.

Then James scrambled up onto the ledge surrounding the roof. Looking down, he pressed the button on his camera, twisted his body to get a better angle, took another shot. He was silhouetted against the blue-black sky. Like he was on the edge of the known world.

Like he was about to fall.

Memories teased the edges of her consciousness.

*A rush of wind.*

*Teetering on the edge.*

*The crunch and slide of gravel underfoot.*

*The sensation of falling.* Sounds hushed, *her surroundings blurred.*

Before she knew it, she was sitting on the cold roof, her head between her knees. Dizzy, nauseated. A sharp throbbing behind her eyes.

"Georgette? Georgie?"

Hands on her shoulders, then warm arms around her. He knelt in front of her. She shivered against him, comforted by his solidity. His warm gaze grounded her. Somehow James had become the center of everything. The one who understood parts of her psyche she didn't even recognize as hers. The one who could put her back together, like Humpty Dumpty. And in this moment, that thought wasn't frightening but just right.

She reached up to touch his cheek. He looked down at her from inches away, and he didn't release her, and she didn't want him to.

She tilted her head, welcoming.

His gaze darkened.

*Yes. Kiss me. Ground me. Wake me up, like Sleeping Beauty from a years-long sleep.* But she didn't say it.

James knew, though. "The first time we kissed, our noses bumped." He touched the end of her nose. "And we didn't know what to do with our chins." His voice was soft. So soft. "You don't remember?"

"I'll remember this time."

His eyes gleamed. "You will." And then he leaned in.

Her eyes fluttered closed, anticipating. And flew open as he rubbed noses with her, laughing softly.

She growled, deep in her throat, and pulled him closer. If he wasn't going to kiss her, she'd have to take charge and do it herself.

The look in his eyes changed, sparked with something more intense.

He kissed her. She kissed him back.

Sitting on the rooftop, he gathered her close, she pulled him closer. She closed her eyes, searching for memory, but felt none. Just the feel of his mouth against her lips, his tongue twining with hers, his rough chin rubbing against hers. Familiar, foreign, shockingly new. A surge of desire stole her breath.

She'd dreamed about this man for six months. She'd captured the high curve of his cheekbones with a few brushstrokes—she caressed his cheek now, relishing the rough stubble. She'd caught the sienna tone of his irises, and the way his eyebrows arched in a perpetual question—she traced that line of eyebrow now, tickled by his nearness, by the tangible reality of this moment. She'd painted *him*. This man.

He opened his eyes and looked down at her quizzically, and she kissed him again, deep and wet and toe-curlingly satisfying. She slipped her hands under his sweater, delighting in the ripple of muscle under skin, loving his responsive inhalation. Her paintings didn't do him justice. She'd tried to catch the strangely vulnerable, outrageously masculine strength that radiated from him, but the charisma, the *heat* of him was so much more powerful in person, she'd never had a chance.

James felt like a teenager again, with heedless lust overwhelming his brain, the surroundings falling away. The only thing that mattered was this. The pulse between them that had always existed, this sexual tension like a live thing.

He pulled her onto his lap, relishing her gasp. He slid his hands under her shirt, seeking the soft curve of breast. She moaned, murmured, "Yes, like that, yes," against his mouth. He wanted more. Wanted her. Here on the chilly roof, among the shadows of the lawn chairs and the jeweled city backdrop. Wanted her in the stairwell, or in the center of the party, or even in that ridiculous, over-the-top slide. Anywhere, any way.

He needed this. Needed to erase the past, create new memories to supplant the bittersweet echoes. Needed to wrap himself up in this woman. This very much alive woman, not the half-dead girl at the bottom of the ravine.

"This is—this is perfect. Absolution and newness and, God, Georgette." He captured her mouth with his, thrusting deep with his tongue. She responded for a brief moment, arching her chest up against him, but then pulled away.

He opened his eyes to find her staring at him. "What?"

"You were there." She slithered out of his lap and stood, sliding her bra strap back onto her shoulder, smoothing her rumpled sweater.

He scrambled up too, feeling like he'd been slapped. "What? Where?" But he knew.

She ran her fingers through her hair, trying to

tame the wildness. He didn't have the heart to tell her she was intensifying that just-had-sex look.

The light from the buildings around them cast a glow on her oval face and the halo of dark, wavy hair. She looked heartbreakingly beautiful. *Modigliani, eat your heart out.*

"'Absolution,' you said. Absolution. You don't want to be with me, you want forgiveness. When you came to me in the studio, you talked about me holding something against you, and how we never saw each other after what happened that day. You were there. Did you see me fall? Did you push me?" Her voice was emotionless. Like she could put it all away into a drawer, shut him away, shut him out.

"It wasn't—I wasn't—" But the look in her eye pinned him, and he had to tell the truth. "Yes. I was there. But you did it to yourself."

After that bombshell, Georgette couldn't look at James again. He tried to talk to her, grabbed her arm, but she pulled away. She couldn't be with him right now. Not after that revelation.

*Past is done.* But it wasn't. Past was a wide-open question mark, filled with unknown pain. And she was terrified of the answer in his all-too-expressive face.

She was halfway out the front door, shrugging into her wool coat, when she remembered. She'd promised to meet up with Hayley and leave together.

She stepped back inside and sent a quick text: *Kill Luka yet?* There. That sounded normal.

*Too many bodyguards. And by bodyguards, I mean bubbleheaded models gushing over his money. Ready to go?*

*Yes. Please.* She felt numb. She could do this. She could act normal.

Her mouth felt bruised, her chin was scraped from his sandpaper stubble, and her body still throbbed in the aftermath of their encounter. Her brain felt thick. Hard to think. Harder to feel.

He'd been at the gorge. He'd witnessed her fall.

No wonder she couldn't remember him. Classic amnesia—head trauma combined with emotional shutdown in a toxic brew.

James had been there.

The worst moment of her life. The moment she'd spent years recovering from. Moving past. And now it was an open pit, and she felt like she was about to fall in.

He'd been there. And he claimed she'd done it to herself.

The thought was untenable. Impossible.

She stumbled and nearly fell, but Hayley showed up in time to steady her.

Georgette nodded her thanks, blinking back tears.

"It's him, isn't it? That guy, James. I'll kill him for you, just say the word."

Georgette gave her friend a weak smile. "I'll let you know." She pushed the door open. The rush of cold steadied her.

Hayley glanced at her, sucking in her lower lip but wisely keeping quiet.

The subway platform was quiet. Hayley leaned against a pillar, yawning. Georgette paced, glancing across the tracks at the other side, the platform going in the other direction.

She saw a familiar figure on a bench.

James, his head in his hands. Looking as somber as she'd ever seen him. Like he might have looked when he'd seen her at the bottom of that chasm ten years ago.

He lifted his head. Met her gaze across the expanse of tracks. Her chest constricted at the pain in his expression.

A train roared into the station, obscuring him from view. When the train pulled out, he was gone.

# Chapter Nine

Two ten a.m. The living room ceiling in Alanna's apartment was unevenly painted—the cream base was overlaid with ragged patches of white where someone must have painted over the cracks in a hurry.

Georgette counted the patches. Tried guessing the length of the cracks underneath. Tried to avoid picturing James on that bench across the darkened rows of tracks, his body curved inward under the yellow-tinted light above the platform. Radiating defeat.

Was that the last time she'd ever see him? It probably should be. And yet...

*No. No more dreams. No more obsessive thoughts. No more James. No more.*

That painted-over crack over there, along the far edge of the wall, it looked like a question mark.

James had been there. Had seen her fall.

She had done a painting, him as a teenager, standing against—standing—his gaze—

*Stop.*

*No.*

*Don't go there.*

Two thirty a.m. Georgette sat at the dining table, wrapped in the comforter, writing a list.

WHAT JAMES MEANT

1) That I tripped
2) That I didn't trip
3) That he wanted to upset me
4) That it doesn't matter
5) That I should stop writing lists
6) That I should stop thinking about him.

Under it, she wrote *Past is done* and underlined it twice. Then circled it for good measure.

She went back to the couch that was her torture chamber of a bed. *No dreams this time. No more memories.*

She closed her eyes. And saw James. The look in his eyes as she pulled away from his embrace. The look as he said, *"You did it to yourself."*

He'd been there. He knew.

She opened her eyes. *James.*

*Dammit.*

Two forty five a.m. The light from the street slanted in the living room window of Alanna's fourth-floor walkup as Georgette donned her long coat over her pajamas, slid her bare feet into her winter boots, then quietly let herself out of the apartment.

The studio was shrouded in darkness, with the paintings casting long shadows across the paint-stained cement floor. A small floor lamp was on, a single point of light. The room was dead quiet, no traffic sounds to break the eerie hush.

Georgette turned the painting toward the light, a shiver like a premonition running through her, but of past rather than future. A teenaged James looked out of the canvas, his taut, muscular body elongated by the low, wide angle view. The sky behind him was the startling clear blue of clean mountain air. The deep green leaves on the trees around him were tipped with the barest hint of autumnal yellow.

And his expression. That was why she'd come, to see that again. His painted visage had that wide, shocked look she remembered from her dream image. Eyes dilated even against the sun. Lips parted like he was about to shout out. Forehead, cheeks creased with pain. Looking at it now, Georgette felt an answering twinge in her gut.

She'd painted that moment. Her last sight before she fell. Could he be right? Had she jumped? Why would she?

She sat on the hard concrete floor, burying her hands in her hair. Pulling on the strands, seeking that pain, that grounding.

Who had she been, this girl who was and wasn't her? What pieces of her life lay in wait in her subconscious? Missing jigsaw puzzle pieces, but jagged, with sharp teeth.

Georgette pulled her phone out of her pocket. The rings echoed in her brain. *Answer. Please answer.*

"H'lo?"

"Hi, Mom."

"Georgette? Are you okay? What's going on?"

"Sorry it's so late. Everything's fine. I wanted to hear your voice, that's all." Georgette touched the canvas leaning against the wall. She traced the bumpy brushstrokes, painted last month during a single weekend—a creative frenzy after a vividly haunting dream. James's face looked so scared. So young. "I'm sorry, I wasn't thinking. Go back to sleep. We can talk in the morning."

Her mother's voice was sharper now, more awake. "What happened?"

Staring at the painting, Georgette said, "You know how I asked you about James earlier?"

"Yes." Her mother sounded strangely wary.

"I ran into him. Here. In New York."

Her mother was silent. Then: "What did he say to you? That boy was always unreliable. You have to know that."

*That boy.* James.

Georgette bowed her head, touching her bent knees with her forehead. "I don't know anything anymore." New Mexico had never felt farther away.

"Oh, sweetheart. It's so late. You must be

exhausted. You're not going to be reacting from a logical place. I'm sure you'll be able to put it all in the right perspective in the morning."

"I'm sure you're right." What else could she say?

After she got off the phone, she went to turn off the lights and leave. But another painting of James caught her eye. She went over to it. This was the real reason she'd come, though she'd chickened out once she got here. She'd been afraid to look. But here it was. And she couldn't look away.

He was sitting on a bench in a desolate subway station, his head in his hands, his posture mournful, as if he'd lost something precious. Exactly the way he'd looked tonight.

All the details were right. His worn leather bomber jacket. The scuffed brown boots peeking out from under his narrow-cut jeans. His hair curling over his ears. Even the deep blue scarf around his neck. It could have been from a snapshot.

Except that she'd painted it two months ago, before they'd even met.

James had stopped outside Albany for a poor excuse for a hamburger and a huge takeout cup of black coffee, then hit the road again, eager to sleep in his own bed tonight. Eager to wash off the road dust, the stink of the city, and, most of all, the too-vivid memories of kissing Georgette.

Four a.m. James pulled into his own driveway. A raccoon bounded away from his headlights as he parked. He turned off the engine and got out. The air smelled like cedar and winter and all good things.

Home.

When the buzzer went off, Georgette was sound asleep. She crammed a pillow over her head and rolled over on Alanna's couch. She'd gotten back to the apartment around five a.m. but had only fallen asleep as the sky lightened toward late winter's dawn.

It rang again. "I'm coming, I'm coming!" Alanna crossed the living room and pressed the intercom. "Who's there?"

"Is Georgette Soren there?"

Georgette sat up, abruptly wide awake. "Mom?"

Alanna raised her eyebrows and pressed the intercom again. "Is this her mother?"

"It is."

Alanna swiveled to look at Georgette. "Should I tell her to go away?"

"Very funny." Georgette catapulted herself out of bed and threw her nightshirt into her suitcase, snagged a new shirt, and hastily pulled it over her head as Alanna buzzed her mother into the building. She didn't want her always-neatly-put-together mother to see her so disheveled and undone.

"You could have told me she was coming." Alanna headed into the kitchenette.

"I had no idea! They're supposed to be spending the holiday at home in Albuquerque, and I'm supposed to be sticking around here, finishing my dissertation and looking for a new apartment." Which she'd do. Next week. Once she cleared her head.

"Huh."

"Yeah. Very out of character. My mom never does anything without her lists and plans and cross-checks."

"Sounds like someone else I know." Alanna opened the fridge.

"Not so much lately." Georgette yanked the blankets off the couch and tossed them behind the armchair.

Someone knocked on the door. Georgette flew to answer it.

Her mother stood there, three-inch heels dangling from her hand and a huge, fake smile plastered on her face. "Breakfast at Tiffany's! Or, well, how about lunch at the Top of the Rock?"

The axe bit into the wood with a satisfying thunk. James left the axe sticking out of the log and shrugged off his winter jacket. Chopping firewood had gotten his blood going. The chill bite in the air felt good on his sweaty back.

His mother trundled the wheelbarrow over to the chopping block and started gathering split logs.

He handed her a log for the pile.

She nodded her thanks, shaking her neat bun out of place. As she pinned it back, she gave him a puzzled look. "Something happened in New York. What?"

"What do you mean?"

"You come over for breakfast, bolt your food in five minutes flat, and take off out the door to work up a sweat on my firewood pile. You're riled up."

"The city felt claustrophobic."

"Bull. You like it there, always have."

He hefted the axe and slammed it into the tree trunk on the chopping block. The wood split cleanly. "I ran into Georgette."

"Did you, now?" She picked up a log from the ground and set it on her growing pile. "That must have been strange." Her tone was flat, as if she was only mildly curious. "Is she healthy?"

"She seems to have recovered fully, if that's what you mean. With one minor exception."

"And what would that be?"

"She doesn't remember what happened at the gorge." He lifted the axe. "Or me." And slammed it into the wood so hard, the handle vibrated violently. "At all."

"How odd."

"You could say that."

His mother regarded him silently for a minute, then went back to filling the wheelbarrow. He went back to splitting wood. His shoulders ached, his legs hurt from the tension of keeping steady, and his hands were getting chewed up. Best way to clear his head. It was good to be home.

Before his mother rolled the wheelbarrow over to the woodshed, she thumped his back. "You'll be fine. You got over her once, after all."

Sally smiled at her daughter over a tall glass of agave-sweetened iced tea, swirling her spoon in the tinted liquid. "I woke up this morning and thought, well, why not? I have those frequent flyer miles, and your father's coming through JFK tomorrow. Let's do the family thing, I thought."

Georgette impulsively reached out past the bread plates and water glasses to envelop her mother's neatly manicured hands in hers. "I'm glad you did."

Gently extricating her hands, her mother nodded, a nod that said, *I understand everything.* She might, at that. "That boy showing up really shook you, didn't it?"

Georgette hesitated. "The things he said…"

"I doubt you can believe anything he said to you."

She took a deep gulp of iced tea. "So what *did* he say?" Her tone was casual, but when she set the glass down, it rattled on the table.

"Not a lot." Kissing under the bridge. The time he spilled a blue drink on her. Sledding—but no, that was her flash of memory. "It sounded like we were together a while. It sounds like it meant something. To both of us."

"Poor boy. I'm sure he believes that. Memory is a funny thing. So unreliable."

Georgette took a deep breath. "It seems like he still feels guilty about my accident."

The words hung in the air between them. Her family rarely talked about the accident. It felt like breaking an unspoken pact to bring it up now.

Her mother dabbed her mouth with a napkin. "Why would he have anything to do with it? You were down at the reservoir, going for a swim on a hot August day. You weren't supposed to sneak under the fence, but all the kids did it. Only this time, you slipped and fell before you got to the watering hole. That cliff down to the water, it's terribly high. Terribly far." Georgette had heard it all before, almost word for word. Her mother balled up the napkin. "It was an accident. It could have happened to anyone. Why would a boy you barely knew have anything to do with that?" But her voice sounded strangled, and she clutched the napkin for dear life.

"Mom."

Her mother blinked rapidly but didn't meet her gaze.

"*Mom*. What aren't you telling me?"

Sally looked up. Her face was wet. "Accidents like that can leave a lasting psychic scar. Your memory loss was a blessing. It was as if it had never happened. No residual trauma. No stress. You're fine now. It's taken a long time to get here, but you're fine. You were alone. You tripped. You fell. It's a miracle you can walk. And that's all there is to it. That's all."

Georgette sat back in her chair, stunned. Her mother, crying. During the hard months of rehab, her mother had been the one who held Georgette while she cried. Sally had been the strong one, seeming to find emotional reserves that nobody knew she'd had. But now…

Her mother wiped her eyes with what was left of the napkin. "Let's plan our day. Do you want to go to the Metropolitan Museum of Art or the Guggenheim first?"

# Chapter Ten

Georgette watched her parents hurry down the street, heading to their hotel. They were bundled up like Eskimos, hunched over as if from a harsh wind, but the weather hovered above freezing and the air was calm. They'd lost their upstate New York hardiness, softened by warm Albuquerque winters.

At the restaurant tonight, her mother had gone to the ladies' room between the entrée and the dessert. As soon as she was far enough away, her father leaned across the black glass table, nearly dipping his elbow into his mashed potatoes. "Honey, I know you feel like you need to know everything. You wouldn't be you if you didn't have that drive, and it's part of what we love about you. But could you leave this one alone?"

Georgette took a sip of wine to steady herself. "Leave what alone?"

"The accident. The reservoir. That boyfriend. The whole thing."

*That boyfriend.* Georgette put down the wineglass.

"It's hurting your mother. She doesn't like to show it, but she hasn't been sleeping well since she got here, and she's waking herself up crying out. She's more fragile than she appears. I don't know how much you remember, but she's had bouts of anxiety in the past.

I'd hate to see her go through that again."

It was true. She remembered her mother weeping at the kitchen table, still dressed in her nightgown when Georgette got home from kindergarten. That was before her mother went back to school to get her own degree and got her life together. Well before the accident.

Her father was right. She couldn't risk her mother's well-being. And she wasn't sure she really wanted to know. And yet somehow she found herself saying, "I know. I do. But I need to know more. This is—I feel like a Band-Aid got ripped off a wound I didn't even know was there. Just... answer a few questions, okay? Can't you do that much?" Because he was here. And he knew more than he was saying. Both her parents did. And that felt intolerable.

He gave the back of the room a furtive glance, then nodded warily. "What do you want to know?"

She hesitated. If he told her something different from their usual story, was she ready for that? But she had to ask. "Why didn't you ever tell me? Did I jump? Was I trying to—to hurt myself? Is that why?"

"Did you *what*? Of course not! This is coming from that boy, isn't it? He's lying. You know that, don't you?"

*Deep breath. Moving on.* "What do you know about James? Me and James, I mean. Were we—was it serious? What *can* you tell me? Anything?"

Her father took his glasses off and rubbed his face, then put them back on. "You don't ask much, do you?" But he said it with a sad sort of laugh. "You were so different that year, practically from the moment you started seeing him. You were wild. Breaking curfew. Fighting with us constantly. And then when you didn't remember... Well. It seemed like a blessing. A do-over."

"And that day? What happened?"

"We think you and he had a fight, and—" He interrupted himself, then started again in a radically altered tone. "So, you're going to be a spa shrink, huh? Never thought I'd raised a granola-head daughter."

Georgette's mother sat down with a rustle of fabric. "Hey, I love Water of Life! It's not all crystals and auras. People who come for their weekend retreats are open to change. They'd get such benefit from our Georgie's insights, don't you think?"

Her father gave her mother a sly grin. "I'm teasing, you know that, right? It's a great job." Her father shifted his smile to Georgette. His gaze held a reminder: *Don't bring up anything difficult.*

When Georgette emerged from the Greenpoint subway station, she found herself heading due west, not northwest. Heading toward the studio, not

Alanna's apartment. She had to see those paintings again. For perfectly sensible reasons. The paintings were images from her subconscious. They might shed light on her father's words.

It wasn't that she wanted to see James's face again. It wasn't that at all.

When she opened the door, expecting quiet, she found Alanna and Miles there. Alanna was gesturing to a canvas leaning against the wall. "But I like this one. It expresses who you are."

"I'm naked. Can't see my parents wanting to hang it over the fireplace."

Alanna giggled. "You may have a point." She looked over at Georgette. "Come here, help us decide."

Georgette unbuttoned her coat. "You're sending a painting to Miles's parents?"

"Driving up to Vermont tomorrow to see them. They keep saying they want to see my work. We thought we could give them a late Christmas present. Which one of these says I'm brilliantly talented and worthy of their son?"

Georgette gestured to the obvious choice. "This one. It's perfect." It depicted Miles standing on the balcony of his one-bedroom apartment in Brooklyn Heights, the sun glinting on the East River behind him, the Manhattan skyline a suggestion of gray and blue and brown rectangles. He looked relaxed, open.

Happy.

Miles raised his eyebrows at Alanna. "See?"

Alanna scrunched up her face. "I guess."

Ah. They must still be arguing about whether she'd move into his place. "It *is* a great apartment."

Miles grinned at Alanna. "Listen to Georgette. She's smart."

"Yeah, maybe." Alanna clearly meant *no*.

Miles bowed his head, like he was trying to make it not hurt. Trouble there.

Alanna turned to Georgette. "Hey, you're here. You ditched your folks. Had enough?"

"We've been to the Met, MoMA, the Whitney, went skating in Bryant Park, ogled the department store displays on Fifth Avenue, and even braved the crowds to see the tree in Rockefeller Center. We exchanged presents last night. They gave me a lovely music box, which I'll have to stash in my storage locker." Georgette went over to the wall with her paintings. "They're leaving in the morning. I'm Christmas in New York-ed out."

She stared at the paintings.

Alanna came up behind her. "Did you ask them about him?"

Georgette grimaced. "As much as they'd let me." Teen James on the cliff edge looked playful, mischievous. Wild? A shiver ran through her.

Miles set the canvas by the door and came over, setting his hands on Alanna's shoulders companionably. "What's this about?"

"Nothing." Georgette gazed at teen James crouching in an empty room, all sharp edges and pain.

Alanna frowned at her but addressed Miles. "Hardly nothing. Turns out Georgette forgot a big chunk of eleventh grade. Including her boyfriend."

Miles's eyebrows shot up. "You mean like amnesia? Does that really happen?"

"It can, yeah. I had a bad fall. Hit my head pretty hard." Georgette touched the scar on her scalp, a reflex. "It's not a big deal."

Alanna snorted. "Yeah, only life-changing, whether or not you admit it." She turned to her boyfriend. "Our friend here is supposed to go digging in her past—go back to the scene of the crime, so to speak—but she's a big old coward and wants to pretend it never happened."

"I'm simply being practical. What if I don't like what I find out? I've done okay these last ten years. Why fix what's not broken?"

Alanna gave her a look. "It's broken. James didn't show up in your dreams for no reason. You need to figure this out. Go to that town in the Adirondacks— what's it called?"

"Pine Mountain. It's easy for Professor Kinsella to

say, sitting behind her messy desk, all clinical detachment and theory. But it's my life. My psyche. What if I discover I'm not who I thought I was?" *What if I did try to kill myself?* "Who do I become then?"

Miles studied her. "You *are* afraid."

"Hell yeah. Wouldn't you be?" Georgette buttoned up her coat. "You know what, I'm going to head back to the apartment. See you guys later."

Alanna moved to block her way. "Ever since I first met you, you've been this hypercalm, insightfully analytical, totally awesome person who keeps it all buttoned up." She gestured at the buttons on Georgette's coat. "Like that. Maybe it's time to unbutton the coat and see what's underneath. What's the worst that could happen? You come back here, we give you big hugs, and you get piles of therapy and stop having those weird dreams. At least you'll know, right? At least you'll be whole."

*Past is done.* The words throbbed in her head, sounding suspiciously like a curse.

It had been her mother's decision to move past the pain. Not hers. She'd never been allowed to make that choice for herself.

"I guess I should do it. I'll go to Pine Mountain."

James crouched on the living room floor. "Don't do it! You're going to—"

But it was too late. He went down in a tumble of limbs as his attacker dissolved into loud cackles. "Got you, Unca Jame, got you!"

He grabbed his pint-size opponent, rolling over with him. "Not so fast, you don't."

Aidan let out a yelp that sounded too much like an incipient wail, so James tickled him, which worked beautifully. His nephew thrashed and giggled and threw his arms around James.

"James, Aiden, Boxing Day lunch, come and get it." His mother was originally from Nova Scotia, and for her, the day after Christmas was almost as festive as the day itself. She'd kept up the tradition after moving to the US.

James picked the little boy up and carried him to the table, which was laden down by a holiday feast fit for royalty, if royalty liked the homey comforts of country hams and meat pies, candied yams and creamed spinach. He looked around the table at his extended family: his two sisters and their respective spouses—Willa and her husband, Sean; Karen and her wife, Gretchen—and their children, then toward his mother at the head of the table, who raised a glass, and everyone else followed suit. Except for Aiden, who wriggled off his lap and ran over to Willa, burying his face in her lap.

For the first time since he'd gotten home, James

felt settled. At peace, even if it was momentary.

He was lucky. He had this. He might never be able to trust his heart to a lover, not like his sisters had, but he had family. Unconditional love.

And maybe now that he'd seen Georgette healthy, if not exactly thriving, he'd finally be able to drive past the reservoir without flinching.

The scenery flashing past—graceful tall pines and stunted balsam fir nestled in a light blanket of snow— was so familiar, it hurt. Georgette had loved living here, relished the intensity of the seasons and the harsh beauty of the mountains. Hard to believe she'd never been back.

In the front seat, Miles and Alanna were speaking in soft tones. "You spend most of your time at my place anyway. Why not have more than a single dresser drawer and a few boxes of hot chocolate mix?" Miles sounded so reasonable, so patient. So clueless. Alanna wasn't going to be persuaded by logic. She needed passion.

Sure enough: "A dresser? I have a whole apartment, thanks. Why would I give that up to move into your one bedroom? Because it has a view?"

"And a better neighborhood."

Georgette suppressed a sigh. *Miles, you're supposed to say, Because it has me. And all it's missing is you.* But he wasn't the type to wear his heart on his sleeve.

Alanna glanced back toward Georgette, as if to say, *See? See what I'm dealing with?*

Georgette leaned forward. "Make a right at this intersection."

Miles turned the wheel. "Should we stick around for a bit? Let you get your bearings before we head out?"

Alanna tilted her head. "I know I said you should do it and all, but if you're not up for this, if it's too much, you can come with us to Vermont instead."

Georgette gave them a wobbly smile. "I'll be okay." *I hope.* "And if not, I'll catch the Greyhound back home tomorrow."

Miles glanced out the window. The sky was an expanse of white. "Assuming a blizzard doesn't come through."

"I grew up upstate. A little snow doesn't scare me. Turn at the next light, past the church."

Alanna whistled as they drove through the center of town. "You grew up here? Norman Rockwell would be rolling around in the street from sheer joy. It's perfect."

Georgette looked around at the old-fashioned pharmacy, the wood-shingled general store, and the clapboard church, painted pale peach. "It kind of is, isn't it?"

Miles turned onto a residential street. "Why did your folks move away?"

"My dad got a job at the best international law firm in Albuquerque. The commute to Utica from here was too much for him, he said. And he and my mom hated the weather." And the dry, warm air was easier on her body, helped with the healing process, but she left that part out. Miles didn't need to know the gory details of her accident and recovery. Nobody did.

"Here it is." Georgette pointed to a sign outside an oversized Victorian, the Blackberry Brambles Inn.

Miles pulled up outside and hopped out to help with Georgette's bag. As he handed it over, he paused. "We'll be at my parents' for a week. Call anytime, and I can come get you."

Georgette took the suitcase. "Thanks, Miles. I hope Alanna knows how lucky she is."

He smiled, a little lopsided. "I'm pushing too hard, aren't I?"

"Maybe a little. But it's good for her. Allows her to confront her fears early in the relationship. You'll get past this speed bump."

"I hope you're right." He gave the suitcase a little pat. "Good luck with your quest."

"Thanks." Georgette squared her shoulders and headed for the quaint, charming building, which felt more like a gauntlet than an inviting vacation spot.

# Chapter Eleven

Georgette rang the bell, then tried the knob. The door swung open, leading to a wide foyer, a small desk set up facing the entrance. Nobody was at the desk.

"Hello?"

An Asian woman in her late twenties emerged from the back, carrying a plate of cookies and accompanied by three large dogs. "Coming!" Her face was familiar. From high school?

As the woman approached, she proffered the plate. "Cookie? Fresh out of the oven. They're for sherry-and-cookies hour, but you can have one."

As Georgette took a cookie, the other woman set the plate down and leaned over the desk, clicking on a computer mouse. "What's your name, are we expecting you? Down, Rocky!" Too late. The Labrador retriever munched happily, if messily, on its stolen treat. The woman sighed. "Your name?"

"Georgette Soren. Good cookie, thanks."

The woman whipped around. Stared. "I'll be damned. It *is* you." Her tone went cold. "What are you doing here?"

"I... What?" And with that, it clicked into place. "You're Kim. Kimberly Li. We were in the same homeroom. I remember hanging out here after school."

Kim frowned. "I hope you're not here to see James Falk. It took him long enough after the last time." The dogs barked. Kim grabbed their collars.

"Are you talking about my accident? Because I hardly think I fell off the cliff to hurt him."

"That's not what I meant." Kim had the grace to modulate her tone. Kind of. "It must have been hell, what you went through."

"It was."

"But why did you ditch him like that after? You froze him out like he was the bad guy. That hurt. I know, I was there. Unlike you." And with that, she was out the door, surrounded by a phalanx of excited dogs.

Georgette stared after her. Maybe she should call Miles for that ride after all. Or find a different place to stay in town. Not that there were many choices.

An older woman came down the stairs. "Don't leave." It was Patsy Li, Kim's mother. No wonder the cookies were so tasty. Patsy had always been the best baker in town.

It felt like a veil over her memory was lifting, like the little facts that were coming back were bits and pieces she'd always known but simply hadn't thought to remember. "Kim was pretty emphatic."

"My daughter the hothead. She's still in love with him, you know. Not that it'll do her any good. But you're welcome here. Georgette, right? I was looking forward to seeing you again. I've thought of you often."

"You have?"

"It broke my heart, what happened to you. The reservoir should be off-limits for kids, but you know how it goes. You ban something and it becomes more desirable, not less." She sat down at the computer and input a few things. "Okay, all set. I'll show you up to your room."

Georgette snagged another cookie and followed Patsy upstairs.

As Patsy opened the room door and handed over the key, she gave Georgette a kind smile. "Breakfast is from seven to nine, sherry and cookies from four to six. Kim will get over her anger, you'll see. It's just that she dated James after you left. He wasn't over what happened. Do you have plans while you're up here? It's the holiday week. Most everything will be closed. The ski runs might be open. I can check for you."

"That's okay." Georgette pulled her suitcase into the room, which was decorated shabby chic and utterly charming, with a distinct lack of ruffles and a preponderance of tasteful antiques. "The truth is, I'm here to remember. I want to go by my old house, the school, the pizza parlor... and the reservoir." She ignored the tightness in her throat. "Maybe that's where I should start."

"Brave girl." Patsy turned to go, then paused. "Do you have a car? I didn't see one on your reservation."

"I thought I'd walk, mostly, and take the bus."

"I'll be driving up over the hill in about an hour to pick up supplies before tomorrow's storm, right past that break in the fence. Want a ride? It's probably the only chance you'll get to see the reservoir. They're predicting a foot of snow tomorrow."

Patsy pulled over on the side of the road, and Georgette opened the door. "Thanks for the ride. I appreciate it."

"I wish I could pick you up on the way back, but I promised Judy I'd stay for dinner. You won't want to stick around here that long."

"I'll be fine. I've got that bus schedule." Georgette proffered it and then put it back in her pocket.

As Patsy drove away down the narrow country road, Georgette turned toward the daunting expanse of untouched snow that lay between her and her goal. Snow and undergrowth and fence.

A foot of snow tomorrow, Patsy had said. She could easily be stuck in town for the rest of her stay. And if she didn't see the reservoir, what was the point?

So she made her way through the snow, brushing past snow-laden branches that showered wetness down on her head, past leafless bushes with twigs that reached out to grab at her coat sleeves with long, stark fingers, until she finally reached the steel-wire chain-link fence with a jagged vertical gash, barely wide enough for one person to slip through.

This fence.

Pushing through, laughing, looking back at—

He was laughing too, reaching out —

If she closed her eyes, she could almost feel the scrape of metal against the bare flesh of her upper arms, the heat of the sun on her back, the fleeting sensation of a kiss...

She pushed the mesh apart with gloved hands to widen the gap, stepped through—

And collapsed onto the ground past the fence, her ankle turned under, her foot caught in a root hidden under the snow.

Gingerly, she tried pulling herself up to stand, clinging to the fence. Sharp pain lanced through her ankle, and she fell again.

Struggling to sit upright, she pulled her cell phone out.

No reception.

The road wasn't visible from here. Nobody would be stopping to pull her out.

She tried to stand again. Couldn't.

Ten minutes. She'd try again in ten minutes. She

couldn't spend the night here.

She started shivering. She wasn't going to cry.

No reason to cry. After all, she'd be able to stand before too long. She'd get out of here. She had to. The alternative was unthinkable.

Pie time on Boxing Day was a multicolored exploration of how berries and squashes and nuts tasted in the family's favorite dessert. Surveying the choices, James felt the first twinge, like the tingle of electricity before a thunderstorm. Something felt wrong.

He glanced around the table. Everyone else seemed perfectly cheerful, chatting and eating and pouring coffee. Except Chester, who sneaked glances at the smartphone under his table and frowned at Gretchen and Karen every time they gently corrected his posture. But that was par for the course with a teen boy.

Ignoring the prickling on the back of his neck, James served himself a slice of eggnog custard pie and one of the mincemeat.

As he took his first bite, the feeling sharpened, a bitter wind chilling his entire body. An involuntary shiver ran through him.

Next to him, Sean glanced over. "You okay?"

"I—" There it was again. Cold and urgency. Like

he shouldn't be here. Like he should be doing something. Not his usual uneasy restlessness, but rather a *do something, dammit* compulsion. He put his napkin on the table and stood, addressing the group. "Hate to eat and run, but I have to go. Something's come up."

Violent shudders raced through Georgette like seizures. Encased in thin city-weight gloves, her hands burned with cold, so she shoved them under the bottom edge of her thankfully heavy winter coat. They buzzed with the returned blood flow. Her neck was exposed. She must have lost her striped wool scarf along the trail. She flipped up the collar of her coat, but there wasn't much more she could do. She still couldn't put any weight on her foot, not even enough to raise herself to stand. She'd tried twenty minutes ago. Ten minutes ago. Five minutes ago.

Her throat was raw from yelling. It was useless. None of the cars she could occasionally hear flashing past on the road would have their windows open to hear her, no matter how loud she screamed. She'd try again anyway. It was all she had.

The problem with following an intuition was that it wasn't a location he could program into his GPS, wasn't a person he could call for directions, wasn't a date on his calendar. It was urgency and cold prickles and confusion.

James backed his car out of his mother's driveway and turned onto the backwoods road—paved last year —and headed toward town. Because he had to go somewhere, so why not there?

Usually the restless feeling subsided when he took action. This time, it grew more intense. His skin felt clammy, as if the frigid air outside was a heat wave. His heart raced for no reason.

He drove.


Georgette hunched over, focusing on her breathing to calm the surges of panic. Puffs of steam in the cold air. She'd been here forever. She'd be here for longer.

Her nose itched. She tried pulling a glove off to scratch it, but the fabric was recalcitrant and her fingers were clumsy.

So sleepy.

So cold.

She put her head on her knees and closed her eyes.


The fastest way to town was on the main road over the mountain, but when James got to the junction, he hesitated at the stop sign. What was he doing out here, chasing a prickling sensation? Probably no more than a low-pressure system ahead of the storm due tomorrow.

He should go on into town, pick up cold cuts and wine, and head home.

He rubbed the back of his neck. It didn't help. Maybe he was coming down with something.

Behind him, a truck pulled up and laid on the horn.

He drove forward. Not left, not directly into town, but the back route. His gut wouldn't let him do otherwise. What was a few miles out of his way? He'd come this far.

It wasn't until he was coasting down the road, his car alone against the stark trees, that he realized—he was about to drive past the reservoir. As he drove past the curve in the road ahead of the path that led to the tear in the fence, the cold prickling became overpowering.

He slowed down. He had to. The sensation was so strong, he might have to pull over.

Because he was driving so slowly, he saw it.

A multicolored striped scarf in the snow. Just like Georgette's.

He swerved and pulled over. When he got out, he saw the footprints. A single set. Small feet. A woman. Going in. None coming out.

The sky was darkening. And somehow he knew. Georgette was in there.

# Chapter Twelve

When they'd met up at the fence that day ten years ago, she'd been wearing a sundress, tight on top with a flared skirt that revealed her legs with every step. The day was hideously hot, but he'd have been flushed anyway, burning up with a mix of longing and fear. His heart had been beating so hard, she could probably hear it.

His heart was beating hard now for entirely different reasons as he followed the tracks through the small stand of trees beyond the road, powering past the branches reaching out to catch him off guard.

There: the expanse of chain links stretching across the clearing.

And there: the jagged hole in the fence, so easy to reach in the summer, slip through and you were there.

But now? He peered ahead—was that…? Oh God. It was. A crumpled heap of a body beyond the fence. Tangled dark hair, long coat, brown boots.

He ran—or rather, tried to run, but the snow caught at his work boots and pulled at his jeans. He waded, clumped, ungainly and too slow. He called, "Hello?" and thought he saw the body stir. *Please let her be—let her—*but he couldn't finish the thought.

"Hello?" He pitched his voice louder.

She sat up slowly. Not unconscious, then. She'd been huddled under her coat, curled in on herself. Her face, a pale oval from this distance, turned toward him. "Thank God." Her voice was slurred.

"I'm coming, hang on!"

He could see her jerk in surprise. "James?"

"I'm here."

She bowed her head, her posture radiating exhaustion and relief.

Cursing the snow, he pushed forward. Finally, he reached the fence. "What happened? Can you get up?" He extended a gloved hand through the fence.

She gripped it, began to rise, then let go, wincing. "My ankle." Her face was twisted in pain and fear. "I can't..." She didn't finish the sentence.

He yanked the twisted mesh with both hands, straining, pushing wide, then leaned his back into one side to keep the gap open. "Kneel and hold your arms up."

She sat, frozen. He'd heard of this. Hypothermia made your thinking slow down.

"Georgette. Listen to me. It's important. Hold your arms up toward me." He demonstrated.

She raised her arms, looking unsure.

He gathered her toward him, ignoring the harsh scrape of the broken fence tearing at his thick jacket. Ignoring the strain on his shoulders, he pulled her through. They collapsed on the snow on the right side of the fence, the side that led to escape.

Now that he held her against him, James could feel the uncontrollable shivers that ran through her like fever chills, wave after wave.

"Let's get you out of here." His voice cracked in two.

She gave a low moan, like an afterthought. "I don't —"

"You won't." He struggled to his feet, then scooped her up, an unsteady Superman tromping through the snow, bringing his fragile-strong Lois Lane to safety.

James nestled Georgette against him on his bed, his arms wrapped securely around her slim form. If he could breathe his body heat into her, he would. Failing that, he'd yanked the comforter off the bed and created a cocoon. He was sweltering under its thick cover, but she still shuddered in violent waves, clinging to him, her eyes closed.

Down the hall, hot water was pouring into the bathtub. That would be the real cure. On his way back here, he'd called Matthias Dahl, his college roommate who was now an emergency room doctor, trying not to sound as panicked as he felt. The nearest hospital was a good thirty miles away, and Georgette needed help immediately. Matthias told him to take deep breaths and talked him through the procedure he should follow.

Now James lifted her in his arms and carried her to the bathroom, still wrapped in the comforter, which trailed behind them in a parody of a wedding train.

When he got to the bathroom, he set her down gently on the thick mat by the tub. She leaned into him, shivering.

"Can you get undressed?"

She fumbled with her clothes, but her fingers were stiff.

He knelt before her. "May I?"

"Please." Her voice was on the edge of tears.

He stripped her quickly, trying not to think about the smooth glide of fabric over skin. Trying not to look. Her body shook, his chest hurt, and he shouldn't notice how damned beautiful she was, not right now. When she was clad in panties and bra, he lifted her and placed her in the tub. She recoiled. "It burns."

"You'll adjust. It's lukewarm."

"If you say so." She grimaced, but her shudders were already diminishing. She sounded more like herself, and he briefly let himself notice the slope of her shoulders rising above the water and the shadowy curve of her breasts underwater, cupped by the wet bra's scant cover.

She shivered, making the water dance, and he looked away, shamed. The sight shouldn't be erotic, not now, not like this.

He stood. "I'll be right outside." He grabbed the comforter and fled.

When he got to the hallway, he sank to the floor, listening to her faint splashes and sighs. Torture and relief.

He'd rescued Georgette. And now she was in his home.

Georgette felt like a mummy. Bundled up in a heavy comforter, dressed in James's sweats, lying on the couch in his cozy living room, her hands encased in a pair of his mittens and her ankle tightly wrapped.

He'd saved her.

In her exhaustion and relief, she almost saw a halo shimmering around him as he knelt by the fireplace, stoking the fire. A thread, invisible but real, seemed to stretch between them, delivering him to her when'd she most needed him.

He shifted a log to give the fire more oxygen, then threw in a handful of kindling. Sparks shot up, and Georgette came back to herself.

No invisible thread, no gauzy halo. Just two people alone in a cabin with dusk rapidly falling, the sky outside turning an ever deeper blue.

She shifted on the couch. James rose from his spot by the fire, his forehead creased with worry. "Are you warm enough? Do you want another blanket?"

"I'm good. Thank you."

He set the tongs down. "If you're sure."

"You've done enough, rescuing me—and thank God for it—but you don't need to take care of me too. If you drive me back to the Brambles, I can take it from there."

"You're not going anywhere, not until you've recovered. Unless you want Kim Li to take care of you. She's not the nurturing type."

He came over but stopped when something crunched underfoot—a thick rectangular page. He paused, looking decidedly awkward. When he picked it up, it became clear: it was a photo. He slid it against his side, hiding it from her view.

So of course she had to ask. "What's that?"

"Nothing important. Do you want another blanket? No, you said you didn't. I'll heat some soup. It's a good idea to warm your insides too." He kept the photo flat against his jeans.

"James."

"It doesn't mean anything." But he handed it to her. Its edges were singed, kissed by fire.

It was a girl. Age sixteen or so. Hair a loose mass of dark waves. Cutoffs and a bright orange tank top.

Hip jutting out, posing flirtatiously, with a smile like she had secrets to share.

She nearly didn't recognize herself.

James turned away. "I'll warm up that soup. Butternut squash with a chicken stock base. You're not vegetarian, are you?"

"James."

"I'll go." He sketched a wave toward the kitchen area, but didn't move.

"If having me here is too hard, after…well, everything, I can…" But he was right. She needed help until her ankle healed. "I can call my friends in Vermont. They could come pick me up tomorrow."

"Tell you what. If your ankle is better tomorrow, I'll drop you off at the inn. If not, I'll bring your things here. It's fine, I have the room."

"That's very generous, but—" She gestured to the photo.

He plucked it from her hand. "It's a chunk of the past. Okay, yeah, I thought about burning it after I got home. But I changed my mind. Don't make too much of it."

"That's like asking a dentist to stop looking at your teeth. I'm a psychologist. Of course I'm going to make too much of it."

"My teeth are fine, see?" He bared them at her in an almost-smile. "So, about that soup…"

"Thank you, that would be great. And no, I'm not a vegetarian."

While James busied himself in the open kitchen on the other side of the cozy cabin, Georgette stared at the photo in her hand. *Who are you, young Georgette? What's going on in your head? Are you in love? Is that why you jumped? Did he break your heart?*

In the kitchen, James cursed as he touched the hot pot handle without a glove, then glanced over at her as if to apologize for his bad language. He knew what had happened that day. More than he'd said, anyway. All she had to do was ask, and he'd tell her.

A shudder ran through her, as if the cold from the reservoir had crept into her bones. Knowing what had happened that day, it felt like crossing a threshold. Who would she be on the other side?

When James carried the tray over to the living room area, laden down with two soup bowls, a hunk of bread, and a tub of butter, Georgette was sitting up, ready to eat. She'd taken off the mittens, probably a good sign.

As he set the tray down, she picked up a copy of *Adrenaline Rush* from the coffee table and leafed through it. "Any of your pictures in this issue?"

He glanced at the cover. "I did a piece about a Venezuelan kayaker."

She flipped to the story, an account of riding dangerous waterfalls, with James suited up and riding alongside Pablo. The shots were better that way, without the usual GoPro fisheye distortion. This was in-your-face footage, with James's cameras housed in waterproof cases and strapped to his chest.

Even now, the sight of the bright yellow kayak against the ice blue water spray brought back that pure joy, that intense focus on here and now. If your mind strayed, you could be dead in an instant.

Georgette traced one of the images with her finger, following the line of the kayak slicing through the waterfall. "You were on shore? With a telephoto lens or something?"

James sat cross-legged on the floor and picked up his soup bowl. "I was in a kayak alongside his."

She set the magazine in her lap.

"What? It's safe. Safe-ish. Semi safe." *Yeah, not at all safe.*

"This is your job?"

"This, and an occasional Polar Bear swim." He indicated her soup bowl. "Eat while it's warm."

Georgette dipped her spoon in the thick orange liquid. "When did you start?" She slanted a thoughtful look from under her eyelashes. Analyzing, sifting. "After the accident?"

He said nothing. What could he say?

"Do you think maybe you've been reliving the experience? Showing you're strong enough, brave enough. That you could have, I don't know, rescued me?"

The familiar bone-deep restlessness took over, a need to plow through snowy woods, to climb, fly, swim, fall—to feel his body, shut down his mind.

He set his bowl down and got to his feet. "Enjoy your soup."

"I'm sorry, I didn't mean to—"

"I'll be back in a while."

Craving cold, craving night, craving silence.

"At least tell me to go to hell. Don't just leave." The firelight flickered across Georgette's prone form, across the handmade comforter cover and the ceramic bowl on the coffee table.

"It's okay. You only said the truth, after all." He grabbed his winter coat, his scarf and hat. Stuffed his sock-clad feet into warm snow boots.

And left.

# Chapter Thirteen

*That went well.*

*Or, y'know, not.*

If Georgette could stand up, she'd go after him. Or would she? Maybe the man needed to be alone. Maybe she should have kept her mouth shut.

The front door closed behind James, not gently but not a slam. So he wasn't angry—or at least, not entirely.

She picked up the copy of *Adrenaline Rush* that had fallen to the floor and read about extreme kayaking as she dipped crusty bread in the sweetly spiced soup.

Then she leafed through another issue, searching for James's byline. She found it on a piece about a group of Australians who parachuted from the top of the Grand Canyon. The images were stunning— human silhouettes against a vast red rock landscape. And James was right, he could only have gotten these image if he were right alongside them. At least they had parachutes. Safer than braving huge waterfalls in a flimsy kayak.

Though what if the parachute failed?

That painting she'd done, one of the earliest dreams—James on the pavement, his body twisted—it seemed less fantastical now. Frighteningly possible.

What a way to make a living.

What a complex man. Risk taker, soup provider. Rescuer, but with the constant ozone of danger surrounding him.

By the time James came back, she'd gone through most of the magazines in the pile, reading the articles he'd been involved with.

As soon as he came through the door, she sat up, putting her magazine aside. "I'm sorry I said that. I was out of line."

He hung up his coat and scarf and came over, peeling off his gloves. "No, I'm sorry. I left you alone when you can't walk. That was badly done."

"Speaking of which, do you have a bathroom on this floor?"

"Can you walk leaning on me?"

"I can try." She threw the comforter off. The shivers had thankfully died down before the meal, and her fingers, toes, and ears didn't feel the burn of frostbite. She was lucky. Extraordinarily lucky.

James reached out. She clung to him, hoisting herself up, her left foot elevated. His close proximity, that delicious cold woodsy smell of him, almost made her retreat back to the couch. But needs must, and she had no crutches.

Halfway across the room, James muttered, "Oh

hell," and lifted her up. His arms were corded wood. She laughed into his neck. "I guess all that exercise is good for you."

"At least it's good for something." He set her down outside the bathroom with painful gentleness.

She kept her arms around his neck for support so she wouldn't topple over—or, worse, land on her bum foot. "Everyone who has a career—and not just a job to pay the rent—chooses it to fulfill a psychological need. You're not the only one."

"You?" His dark eyes were filled with some strong emotion, but guarded, like he didn't quite trust her not to hurt him.

"Me most of all. Budding psychologist here, remember? Physician, know thyself."

His gaze softened. He held her elbows for support. She moved inside the bathroom, clutching on to any surface that would support her. He stood outside the door.

She looked in the mirror, then wished she hadn't. Her face was pale, her hair wild. She didn't look like herself. She didn't look tame.

So she kept talking, mostly to the reflection in the mirror. "I'm trying to find a way into the mess inside my head. The missing bits, the bits that make no sense, the bits that don't fit with the other bits. It's always felt like a huge, scary mystery, even before you showed up

—something my family never talked about because the past was done and nobody should dwell in that pain. I plastered over the gaping hole with cognitive behavior therapy and inner-child work."

"Did it work?" His voice was soft from outside the bathroom door.

"I thought so. Until I started therapy as part of my PhD program. She poked and prodded at the memories I did have. Then the dreams started, creating a crack in the facade. You came along and ripped it wide open."


James slept fitfully. Wind rattled the house, the radiator groaned and went silent, and Georgette Soren was sleeping in the next room under a bedspread his sister had picked out of a catalogue.

Half-asleep, he dreamed of the softness of Georgette's skin, the feel of her body in his arms, her clean scent enveloping him. As he fell deeper into sleep, his defenses down, he dreamed of kissing her, caressing her face, cupping her breasts, working his way down her body…

At first her cries sounded like the wind through the trees, a backdrop for his half-waking dreams. But then she shouted out, indistinct but clearly her, and he was instantly awake. He threw off the covers and bolted into the guest bedroom.

When he got there, she was thrashing helplessly, the comforter wrapped around her so tightly, it straitjacketed her arms. Her face was twisted, pained, in the grip of a nightmare.

He knelt by her side, untangling her arms. She moaned—low, wordless. He rubbed her back. She heaved a big sigh and stilled.

But when he started to rise, she whispered, "Don't go."

"I thought you were asleep." He resumed his soothing circular motions on her back, feeling the supple muscles through the thin cotton of his old T-shirt. "Rough dream?"

"I was falling."

His fingers spasmed, catching on the shirt fabric. Was she starting to remember?

"It wasn't like what I'd imagined. No rushing wind or terror." Her voice was dreamy, half-asleep. "Swirling blue sky, endless sky, green-and-brown cliffs, dizzy. There was some fear, I think—"

"You sounded like it."

She buried her face in the pillow. "Sorry."

"No. It's okay. I'm glad." To his surprise, he meant it.

The wind buffeted the house. Trees creaked outside under the weight of new-fallen snow. The night sky outside the window was tinted red. And

Georgette closed her eyes.

James stood, trying to be as quiet as possible, feeling the way he used to when he rocked his oldest nephew, Chester, to sleep when he'd babysit for his sister. Like if he stepped wrong, he'd have to start the whole process again.

He must have stepped wrong.

"James." Georgette's voice was plaintive.

He turned.

"I'm probably going to deny this in the morning, so don't remind me, but…can you lie down with me?"

He froze. Stunned into motionlessness, but his entire body jolted awake. "I don't think that's a good idea."

"You're right. Never mind."

He was halfway to the door when she spoke again. "It's just that every time I close my eyes, I feel like I'm back there. At the fence. Stuck. Like I'll never be warm again." Her voice wobbled, vulnerable with night and trauma.

He went back to the bed, sat down beside her. She slid over. The edge of her face was limned in the reflected light; the rest was darkness.

He lay down, not touching her.

She threw the comforter over him and snuggled up against him.

All his muscles went tense. Blood and energy

suffused his body. Restlessness didn't begin to express it.

Where should he put his arm? If he settled it on her side, the most natural place for it, his hand was millimeters away from her lush breasts. He slid it between their bodies, trying to create a wedge, but all too aware of the inward curve of her supple back, splaying out to firm buttocks below. She wasn't wearing underpants, and the T-shirt he'd given her was hiked up under the sheets. Her skin was burning up, or was that him?

He sat up. "I can't do this."

Georgette opened her eyes, blinking sleepy puzzlement. "What?"

"Unless you want to become lovers tonight, I can't sleep in the same bed with you."

Her mouth opened, but no sound came out.

"Right." He turned and left the room, trying to tamp down the chaotic mix of lust and loss that threatened to drown him.

Now she was wide awake. Her nerve endings had zinged to life after James's last words, their meaning pounding in her veins. Make love in this bed. Now.

Her skin tingled. The sheets felt rough-soft on her exposed lower back, the comforter hot on her legs. She threw off the covers.

She heard James's footsteps in the hallway. Was he coming back? Was he going to ask her if she wanted to, if she would, if she—

She couldn't. Not with this man, not with the constant feeling of danger thrumming under the surface. What he might do, what he might have done. What lay between them unsaid, unknown. Did she want to know, did she want to—

Oh hell. She shifted again. The cool air in the room prickled her oversensitive skin. Her body throbbed. If he came in here, she'd say yes, and damn the consequences.

His footsteps receded down the stairs. Moments later, the front door latched behind him.

It was four a.m. and well below freezing outside. Where was he going? Off to climb a mountain with grappling hooks and nothing else? Or go bungie jumping off the cliff edge with rubber bands tied together in a makeshift rope?

Georgette rolled over and looked out the window. Tiny flakes were falling fast, lit from above by a half-moon. The driveway was invisible, buried beneath the snow that had already fallen tonight. James emerged from the small shed behind the house, carrying a hefty shovel, and set to work.

She envied him.

# Chapter Fourteen

Steeling himself, James knocked on the bedroom door.

"Come in."

He swung the door open. Georgette was sitting up in bed, her foot propped up on a pillow, paging through her smartphone. She gestured out the window. "I forgot how complete snowstorms are up here. It's like the world's been erased." She gave him a quick glance, then averted her eyes, as if the sight burned her. He knew the feeling.

"Yeah. About that." He couldn't quite look at her either. "I don't think I can take you to the inn today. Or even get your suitcase. Until the roads are plowed, we're not going anywhere. Unfortunately, our little road isn't top priority."

"I'll stay out of your way." She still couldn't look at him, and her posture was ramrod straight.

Dammit, this wasn't going to work. He leaned against the wall, arms folded. "Look. I'm not going to attack you. I know what I said last night, but that was —I'm over it, okay? We'll be fine. I'll call my mother. Her house is a quarter-mile walk cutting through the back way. I can get some clothes for you."

His shirt had slid down on one side, revealing her

delicate shoulder. Meeting his gaze, she yanked the neckline, pulling it back up. "That would be good, thank you."

"Have you tried putting weight on your ankle yet?"

"I've been scared to try." She gave him a rueful look, but as soon as their eyes met, she flushed and looked away. Then circled back, looking him full-on for the first time since he'd entered her room. She exhaled. "This is ridiculous. I'm sorry. We're snowbound, trapped for who knows how long. You're being absolutely amazing."

"No more than anyone else would do, given the circumstances."

"I don't know about that." She swung her legs over the edge of the bed. About to put her weight on the foot.

He strode forward, catching her elbows. "Don't. You could damage the healing. Tendons are delicate."

She leaned against him, her weight half on her right foot and half on him. It felt so good, he wanted to stand like this all day. Her scent was the same as it had been ten years ago. Not perfume, just soap and skin. Georgette. His Georgie.

Georgette open to him, needing him. Georgette tender and vulnerable in a way she hadn't been since they'd met again, maybe not ever.

Georgette was his kryptonite. And he was about to explode.

His mother was right. This meticulously analytical yet strangely impulsive woman with her expressive dark eyes and her lush lips and the thoughtful tilt of her head—this woman was going to break his heart if he gave her the chance.

Ensconced on the couch again, its crevices and pillows the contours of her world, Georgette stared balefully at the scallops of snow on the window ledge. She was clean and well fed and trapped in a house with a man who—

Resented her presence? The look in his eyes last night as he turned away. *"Unless you want to become lovers tonight..."*

No, not resented. Not exactly.

A man who carried guilt in the slope of his shoulders. A man who skydived and kayaked and who knew what else, living life along the razor's edge.

She was starting to understand the shiver of restlessness that seemed to overtake him sometimes. Outside, the scrape of the shovel into snow and asphalt driveway told her James was at it again, clearing the long driveway from his house to the road. She swung her legs over the side of the couch and gingerly put a tiny bit of weight on her bad leg. Pain shot up her calf.

Great. She was stuck on this couch without her computer, her notes, or her textbooks.

She pulled out a photo album from under the coffee table and leafed through pages of portraits: sensitive studies taken on his world travels, with locals posing for the camera or holding gear. Some were behind-the-scenes candids of the work that clearly went on to prepare for one of his dangerous shoots.

A second photo album had a series of black-and-white portraits, with lovely soft lighting and clear affection for his subjects. With a start, Georgette recognized one of the women—her old friend Teresa Martinez, now grown into herself, her long black hair pulled back to reveal her fine bone structure. Teresa had been the first kid to truly welcome Georgette to Pine Mountain, back in seventh grade. They'd eaten lunch together under the tree in front of Teresa's house every day that summer, pretending they were royalty, summoning subjects and summarily executing them on a whim. And laughing. A lot.

Georgette's throat clogged. She hadn't even thought to reach out to her old friend. She'd lost more than her memories of James when she'd left Pine Mountain behind. She'd lost part of her life.

She turned the page to a portrait of Kim Li in front of the inn, looking coquettishly at the camera, holding out a treat for an overeager border collie.

They'd been lovers, Kim and James. The thought shouldn't hurt.

Georgette quickly flipped to the next page. The rest of the images were clearly of his family. The resemblance was too striking—those dark eyes, dark hair, slashes of eyebrows. The whole family had the strong features of hardy New Englanders. Black Irish.

Two sisters. One with her husband, the other with her wife. And their mother, the clan matriarch, an older woman with short-cropped dark hair and James's familiar quirked smile.

There were also a number of richly saturated images of the local area. A clearing in the woods, the trees casting long afternoon shadows on gold-tinted forest floor. A springtime shot looking down Main Street, the church steeple visible in the distance, with magnolias, dogwood, and cherry trees in full, glorious bloom.

Beautiful, magical Pine Mountain.

Her phone buzzed. She pulled it out from the couch crevice where she'd tucked it for safekeeping. The message was from Alanna, succinct and to the point:

*So?*

Georgette wrote back: *So what?*

*Have you found out anything yet? More important, have you run into James the Mystery Man? Is the town deadly dull? Do you want us to rescue you yet?*

Georgette laughed, a welcome lightness blooming in the middle of her chest. *You might say I've run into James. I'm staying with him.*

Seconds later, her phone rang. "You're what? How did this happen?"

"I, uh...twisted my ankle."

"What? Are you okay?"

Georgette looked down her blanket-wrapped body at her foot encased in an ACE bandage, a block of ice nestled next to the offending ankle. "Think so. I will be, anyway."

"So how did a busted ankle land you a stay Chez James?"

"He's taking care of me. Wrapping my ankle. Feeding me." *Rubbing my back. Avoiding lying down with me.* "I planned to go back to the inn today, but last night there was a huge storm." Georgette glanced outside. The ledge was heavy with piled snow. "Looks like I'll be here another day or two."

"You're snowed in? Together?" Over the phone, she could hear Alanna suck in her breath. "Have you had sex yet? Please tell me you had monkey sex in front of a roaring fire in the middle of the snowstorm."

Georgette choked. "He's my host. I'm taking enough advantage of his hospitality as it is."

Alanna made a rude noise.

"It's complicated, okay?"

"Does he want you? Do you want him? Make it uncomplicated. Have fun."

If it were only that simple. The idea of sex with James felt like free fall, with no idea what lay at the bottom. "What about you? Shouldn't you be off building snowmen with lover boy? Igloos you can move into together?"

Alanna blew a big sigh into the phone. "You suck, you know that?"

"That's my job. To ask the hard questions."

"No talk about moving, thank God. Seriously, if you feel like you have to flee, let me know. We can work something out. Come rescue you."

"You'd need a sled with a dozen huskies to get here, but thanks. I'm good."

After Alanna disconnected, Georgette cradled her phone, tempted to call her friend back and tell her everything. The reservoir fence. Crouching in the snow, huddled under her coat, convinced she'd freeze to death, nobody discovering her body until spring thaw. Hearing James's voice through the fog filtering into her brain. His arms around her, giving warmth, giving life.

But it felt too fresh to share. Too raw. And, in a way, too intimate.

An unviewed photo album still rested on her lap.

Georgette opened the heavy ivory cover slowly, half-eager and half-afraid to find out what hid beneath its binding.

The first page was empty. There was a lighter rectangle in the center, like a photo had been there, and the edges of the page were bent, implying that someone had removed it clumsily. She turned the page. And then the next. And the next, fanning through the pages, her heart racing.

Nearly all the photos were of her. A much younger version, someone she nearly didn't recognize. Oh, she remembered the green skirt in one shot, the denim jacket in another, the dangly turquoise earrings in a third. The way she used to wear her hair, the way she still tilted her head, even the smear of paint on her cheek in one shot.

But her demeanor in these pictures, that was entirely unfamiliar. Laughing, teasing, running across a meadow barefoot. Sitting astride a motorcycle, for God's sake. And the photos were gorgeous. Taken by someone with a perceptive eye and a full heart.

After Georgette looked at all the pictures, she flipped to the beginning. This girl in the photographs, the boy behind the camera—they'd been in love. What had happened?

It was time for them to talk about that day at the reservoir. Past time. No matter how hard it might be.

No matter what it brought to the surface. Past wasn't done after all. Her memory gap wasn't a blessing. She needed to know or she'd never be able to move forward. And James held the key.

With that thought, as if she'd conjured him, the door opened. James stamped snow off his boots on the mat inside the door, then stripped them off and came in the rest of the way.

Georgette sat up straight. "We need to talk."

"Not right now."

"James. Now."

He gave her a warning look, then turned to the door and beckoned someone inside. Oh.

The older woman from the photo. His mother. She wore a full-length down coat, with a thick knit hat pulled over her graying hair and oversized snowshoes adorning her feet. The epitome of a rugged mountain woman.

She hauled a duffel bag inside, along with a pair of crutches. She let the bag drop onto the floor and set the crutches against the wall. "Barely used. Surprised I still have 'em." She still hadn't acknowledged Georgette's presence.

James brought the crutches over to Georgette, waving one in the air. "A present. For you." He grinned like it was a grand surprise.

His mother, meanwhile, was looking between

them, eyes narrowed.

Two choices presented themselves: let the woman keep acting like this, or call her on it.

Georgette gave her as sweet a smile as she could muster. "Thanks so much for the loan. I'll be glad to be mobile again. Take some of the burden off your son."

James's mother grunted.

Georgette gritted her teeth. "I'm Georgette Soren, but I'm sure you remember."

The older woman gave her a cool once-over. "Yep, I remember. But you don't, he says. Go figure." She dug in her backpack and handed James a couple of Rubbermaid containers. "Thought you might not be prepared for the storm. Brought you some provisions."

James took them reluctantly. "Thanks, but you didn't have to do that."

"Gotta eat." His mother eyed Georgette. Tiger mom? Try rabid grizzly bear mom with huge snowshoes incongruously strapped to her paws.

Georgette smiled at her. Or tried to. "James has been amazing. He rescued me yesterday, did he tell you?"

"Yep." A woman of few syllables.

"I imagine you have a lot of questions. I know I would in your shoes." *Or, uh, snowshoes.* "Like what I'm doing here." *Shut up, Georgette. Don't give the woman rope to hang you.* "I'm hoping to remember that time in my life, when I lived here. I have…gaps."

James winced.

His mother stood stoic. Like a boulder. "Did it work? Do you remember?"

How much to say? She settled for: "Not much, not yet."

"You don't remember how much your rejection hurt him, do you? But you wouldn't. Because you were gone by then." Her voice was caustic.

On second thought, Georgette preferred the silent treatment.

"I'm sorry, I don't. I didn't know." *Screw it.* "No, you know what? I was in a coma for two weeks. Seven months of intensive rehab before I could walk normally. I had to be taught the fine motor skills to brush my teeth and tie my shoes. I cried a lot, but I did it." She gripped the photo album for comfort. "You know what else? I didn't leave James on purpose. My parents moved to New Mexico because it was easier on my body to be somewhere warm and dry. I didn't remember James because the accident stole my memories. And I didn't think about what I might have left behind, about any possible holes in my memory, because I had other things on my mind. It was hard enough getting over the trauma without those images to haunt me too." She grabbed the crutches and began the process of levering herself up. "Nice to see you again. Your son is a good man. You raised him well."

Muscle memory took over, and she swung the crutches out, made her surprisingly speedy way to the bathroom, and pushed the door closed with one crutch, then sat on the closed toilet seat and tried to stop shaking.

# Chapter Fifteen

His mother gave him a look from under her ridiculous knit cap. "She's still got guts, anyway."

"She's got a lot more than that." James gave his mother a kiss on the cheek. She looked surprised. "Thank you for the food. We'll heat it up for lunch. But now, if you'll excuse me…" He glanced toward the closed bathroom door.

"Don't do it."

He frowned. "Don't do what?"

"Have sex with her."

"She's got a busted ankle. We're snowed in. That's all."

She snorted. "Keep telling yourself that. I saw the way you looked at her. You're not a man who loves lightly. You're like your father that way. Can you picture her sticking it out with you here? Last time, when she left, when your letters came back unopened and her phone was disconnected…" She shook her head. "I don't want to see you go through that again."

James clenched his jaw. His mother meant well. She'd seen him at his lowest. "Didn't you hear what she said? Everything she had to deal with? Cut her a break."

"Be careful of your heart, that's all I'm saying." She

grabbed his hands. Her wool mittens felt scratchy against his palms. "Promise me that you'll be careful, at least."

"I promise." The words tasted bitter. Probably because she was right. He was in too deep, and Georgette wasn't right there with him. How could she be? She didn't even remember him.

The murmured conversation from the living room was muffled by the door, but the cadence was clear. James's mother was telling him Georgette was trouble. James sounded uncertain. That was something.

After a few minutes, the front door closed. Had James left with his mother, off to climb mountains and ford frozen rivers?

No. His footsteps came closer. He rapped on the bathroom door. "She's gone. You can come out."

She pushed the door open with the end of her crutch. "I'm sorry I lost my temper."

"I'm sorry my mother is still holding a grudge from ten years ago."

She swung out of the bathroom on the crutches and struck out across the room, a brave adventurer thwacking her way through the living room underbrush back to the couch.

James paced her. "You're good with those."

"I've got experience." She lifted a crutch up to

avoid snagging the edge of the rug.

"What you said to my mother—I never thought about how hard your recovery process must have been. Obvious in retrospect. But the last time I saw you, you were unconscious when the copter airlifted you to the hospital, and the only thing I could think about was whether you'd wake up."

She reached the couch and sat, grateful for its solidity. Facility with crutches was one thing. Comfort was a different matter. Her armpits already ached.

Unexpectedly, James knelt on the rug, his face just below eye level. "Your parents wouldn't let me visit you after the surgery. They told the nurses not to let me in." His tone was carefully neutral. "They blamed me. And then, days after you woke from the coma, you were gone. Off to New Mexico with no forwarding address."

"They blamed you?" Her father: *We think you had a fight.* "But you said—" Her voice wobbled and cracked. She tried again. "You said I did it to myself. What happened at the reservoir? How did I fall?"

He laced his fingers through hers on the edge of the couch. His grip was so tight, it crunched her fingers. "We'd broken up. Did I tell you that?"

"Did you break it off?"

"You did. Your parents gave you a come-to-Jesus talk. You snuck out one last time and told me it was over."

Her father: *"You were so different that year. Wild. Breaking curfew."* "Did they think you were a bad influence?"

His hand slipped away from hers. "Was the working-class boy with a motorcycle and a string of absences from school a bad influence on the A student? What do you think?"

His pain... "I can't apologize for something I don't remember."

"I know. Of course." He was silent for long enough, she thought he was done. He wasn't. When he spoke again, his voice was hoarse. "You sounded so cold that night, like love was a switch you could shut off." He ran his hands along the rug, pushing against the nap, leaving a trail of tufts in their wake. "We were broken up for a couple of months, avoiding each other around town. And then one day, you bumped up against me in line at Carvel's and whispered, 'Meet me at the reservoir tomorrow.'"

James's hands stilled. "You blew me a kiss as you walked away with Teresa. I thought we were getting back together. I thought..." He struggled to his feet. "I'm sorry. I can't do this. Are you hungry? It's lunchtime."

"James." She used the arm of the couch to lever herself up. But he was there, his hand under her elbow, supporting her. She leaned into him, relishing his warmth, though she had no right to that illusion of closeness. "James," she said again.

He made a murmur like assent.

She turned in his arms, feeling his support, a tangible thing, and kissed him. On his forehead. On one cheek, then the other, like a blessing. Then his mouth. Those mobile, expressive lips.

He stilled under her touch. And then he kissed her back. They dropped to the couch—gently, in slow motion. They kissed in slow motion too, tongues tangled sweetly and hands stroking hair and touching cheeks, softness and warmth and healing.

He spoke against her mouth. "You kissed me that day. At the gorge. You ran up to me and kissed me, and I thought... But then you danced away, right at the edge of the cliff."

"So it was an accident?"

He leaned his forehead against hers. Georgette felt the tremor that passed through his body. "You said, 'I brought you here to show you this.' I didn't understand. A breeze caught your sundress, teased your hair, and you were so, so beautiful. I thought you were going to—but then... It was... Seeing you at the bottom..." His voice was rough, halting, and then he stopped talking altogether.

The image painted by his words felt strangely

distant, like someone else's dream, impossible to fully picture. "I jumped? On purpose?"

He closed his eyes. "I don't—it was—" He paused. "I'm sorry. That's all I've got. I'm sorry."

Cupping his face in her hands, she kissed him gently again and again, murmuring between kisses, "I'm alive. I'm okay. I'm here."

At some point, it would start to feel real. At some point, maybe she'd understand who that girl had been, why she'd done that. At some point. Not now.

The first time the knock came, James ignored it. He had Georgette in his arms on the couch, her body pliant against his, her breath coming in gasps mingled with subvocal purrs that raced through his body. And he was sixteen, drowning in sensation and desire, but he was also twenty-seven, fully aware of exactly what they could do next. This time, he didn't think she'd stop him.

Whoever it was could go away.

The second time the knock came, Georgette pulled away. "Shouldn't you get that?"

"Nope." He kissed her again, capturing her lips with his. "They can leave a note."

"But we're snowed in."

She was right. With great reluctance, he disentangled himself and sat up. "Hold my place."

She buttoned her shirt—a soft flannel plaid that had to be his older sister's—and gave him a look that suggested she was already having second thoughts. Dammit.

He went to get the door.

His nephew Chester came in, stamped the snow off his boots, and flung his hood off. "I almost left, except that I saw smoke from your chimney. Could you have been any slower? I think my fingers are about to snap off one by one, and then how will I play hockey? Assuming I ever get off this godforsaken mountain." He went to the pellet stove in the corner and warmed his hands. Then, finally, he noticed Georgette. "Who are you?"

She casually combed her fingers through her hair, as if she'd been taking a nap. Her shirt was buttoned up all the way, thankfully. "Georgette Soren."

"I know *that.*" Chester sounded impatient. "My grandma said. But who are you to my uncle and what are you doing here in a snowstorm? When I asked, she got squirrely and didn't answer. So?"

James intervened. "That's no way to talk to a guest of mine."

Chester flopped down on the rug, his still-jacketed arms flung out. "I'm never getting out of here. The least you could do is amuse me."

Georgette exchanged glances with James. She

started to say, "I knew your uncle—" and James simultaneously said, "So what are you—"

James glanced at Georgette, who nodded for him to take over. "What are you doing here, anyway? Come to spy for my mother? Do I need to pat you down for a wire?"

Chester stared up at the ceiling. "This is a weird ceiling. Do you ever wonder if it's going to fall in?"

James glanced up. It was an arch of multicolored stained wood with exposed beams. He loved it. "Did you come over for a reason?"

"Grandma wants you to come to her New Year's Eve thing tomorrow night."

"I was planning to."

Chester raised himself up on his elbows and pointed at Georgette. "I mean her."

Georgette raised her eyebrows. "Me?"

"Grandma wants you to come specifically. Said that obviously it's contingent on if you can walk that far, but she hopes so."

"Did she say why?"

"Something about gumption and sass. Dunno. Seems like she could have called. I don't know why she had to send me over." James knew. His mother was experienced with teenage angst and was trying to cure Chester's with a long walk in the snow.

Chester stood. "Gotta get back. She'll have more

stupid chores for me. Dude, I don't know how you survived adolescence here."

James grinned. "Got in trouble. Kept her busy chastising me. It worked like a charm." He glanced over at Georgette, who was contemplating him with her therapist expression, like she'd been handed another piece of the puzzle. "Don't make too much of it. I was being a teen boy."

"Mmm."

Chester stopped in the doorway. "So you coming or not?"

Georgette slid her finger underneath the ACE bandage and scratched her ankle. "If I can walk. And if I'm still staying here."

James glowered at her. "Of course you're staying. Where are you going to go? The Blackberry Brambles Inn, with those rickety stairs? You think that's a good idea?"

"Besides, I'd have to be looking behind me all the time, in case Kim decides to give me a little shove."

Chester's eyes lit up. "Who's Kim?"

James pushed him out the door. "Go. Tell my mom we're on. And tell her to be nice."

After he locked the door behind Chester, he retreated to the kitchen. Georgette still looked thoughtful, and he didn't plan to be on the receiving end of her Psych Interrogation Techniques. Not again.

He opened the fridge and gave it a cursory once-over. "I can unfreeze some lamb stew. It's from a few weeks ago. Before I came down to New York." Before everything changed. "Or scramble some eggs, throw in bacon. Or we can chance my mother's casserole, but I should warn you, the hospital's over in Saranac Lake."

"Eggs sounds good." Georgette seemed distracted. "Your nephew. Chester, right?"

"Yeah." James set ingredients on the counter. Eggs, butter, tarragon, mushrooms...

"He's not happy."

"He's missing hockey practice. They were supposed to be back in Albany today."

"It's not just that. Something's bothering him."

He turned the flame up on the front burner and set his favorite cast-iron pan on to get warm. "Teen-boy moodiness. Don't overanalyze."

Behind him on the couch, he could hear Georgette shifting. Rewrapping the bandage. "You know that's what I do, right? Analyze?"

"I know." Itchy restlessness. Muscles clenching, needing release. After lunch, he'd go shovel a path... somewhere. "And that's fine. But sometimes a kid is a kid."

"Like we were?"

Damn and ow. The butter sizzled in the hot pan, sparks flew up, liquid fire spattering his wrist. He turned the faucet on high and shoved his wrist under it. "Not like us." No more interrogations. No more painful memories. Not right now. He wasn't ready to dig any deeper.

After lunch, James went out to shovel, and Georgette settled on the couch with some scholarly articles she'd asked James to print out. Predictably, ten minutes in, she started to yawn. Twenty minutes in, she decided to close her eyes for a moment. To clear her head. So she could absorb the technical details better.

An hour—or more—later, she rose slowly to awareness, to a clicking sound near her ear like a mechanical insect. Or a camera with an old-fashioned shutter.

She opened her eyes. Yep. A camera. Big lens, solid camera. "Watch where you're pointing that thing."

James lowered the camera. "Should have asked?"

"Don't you think?"

"And interrupt your beauty sleep?" He showed her the back of the camera, his fingers sliding through the images.

Her sleeping face, half-silhouetted, half-lit. She looked like that? That pretty?

A close shot of her hand resting on the sheaf of papers, fingers softly curved, an implicit promise.

A shot taken from across the room, rays of light streaming through the window like a caress.

"Not bad. You don't have to delete them." They were more than *not bad*. They were gorgeous. "You're a hell of a photographer."

He sat in the armchair, camera cradled in his hands. "Glad you approve."

She sat up, swinging her legs over the edge of the couch. Gingerly, she tested her foot and felt a twinge, but not the stabbing pain from yesterday. "New shots for your photo album of me. Bet you never expected that."

"Good thing I've got a few extra pages to fill." His gaze met hers, and she could see the wary wonder.

This tentative tenderness between them. The hush of a snowy landscape outside. The crack of a log in the fireplace, the hum of the pellet stove whirring in the corner. In a few days, she'd be gone, back to the city and this would be a few pictures to add to a photo album under his coffee table. And she'd have...

She flipped over the top printout page and did a quick sketch with the number-two pencil she'd been using to make notes. A gesture drawing of James, his arms akimbo, elbows on his knees, camera in his lap. Leaning forward toward her, the guarded yearning in his body more than his face.

James went still, letting her draw. She filled in

details—slashes of cheekbones, eye shape tilted down at the edges. A beauty mark on his cheek. All the elements she'd painted, but never from life. "Did I ever draw you? In high school?"

"A couple of times, yeah. You said I was hard to draw." His mouth quirked. "Claimed I was a puzzle wrapped in an enigma. Happy and mournful."

"Teen me was pretty smart." She filled in shading on his face, angling her pencil so she could use the side of the point.

"She was." He watched her for a moment. "Twenty-seven-year-old you is pretty smart too."

His lips weren't quite right. She erased the edges and drew them again with more care, glancing between his real mouth and the page. That mouth promised so much. A passionate mouth. Made for laughter. Made for…

Her pencil stilled. James was still watching her, his gaze intent, the air between them imbued with an electric charge.

*His hair. Draw his hair.* Swept up off his face today, a casual disarray. His clothes. Those were safe, soft folds of sweater hinting at the muscular torso beneath. *Okay, maybe not so safe.*

"Can I ask you something?"

*The answer is yes. Whatever you want.* "Sure."

"Why aren't you a professional artist? Is it that you

think you're not good enough? Because you are."

Georgette's pencil snagged on an imaginary irregularity in the page. "It's not that." She focused on the camera. All clean rectangles and circles and knobs. Safe. Except for the way his hands cradled the molded plastic, like it was an extension of his body. Or a lover.

*So much for inanimate objects.* "I don't have the temperament. You have to be a risk taker, willing to go long periods without selling a single piece. It's too stressful. I'd rather have a solid career and paint on the side. And someday I might use art in my therapy sessions. It's good for working with kids—they open up more when they're doing something. Drawing, making music, playing sports."

"You like working with kids?"

"Very much." She felt an unexpected pang, thinking of Trudy. "They're in such a vulnerable time. A real connection with an adult can make such a difference. Maybe at some point, I'll work with them full time. Not to start, though. My mother's lined up a good job for me at a New Mexico spa."

"Is that why you're a psychologist? So you can be like your mother?"

It stung. "Hardly." Well, if you discounted the spa job and the lists they both loved and... well. Their mutual career path. "I like helping people. It's as simple as that." The pencil flew across the page. Maybe she could turn this into a painting. The final image of her James series.

"Mmm." Like a good therapist, James left it at that, leaving her to fill in the gap left by his silence.

"Maybe it's also about everything that happened when we were teens. That kind of thing leaves a scar. Which is one of the reasons for amnesia, did you know that? The brain shields itself from memories it's not ready to absorb."

"Are you ready now?" James leaned forward, tilting his body toward her as if he was about to come over.

"Damned if I know." Georgette waggled her finger at him. "Back the way you were."

He settled back into position with a vaguely guilty expression.

# Chapter Sixteen

Over a dinner of leftover stew and freshly cooked potatoes and chard, Georgette was a model guest, asking about his family, who she didn't recall at all, and about the various people she did remember from Pine Mountain—everyone from her high school best friend Theresa to the forever irritable Ahmed, the town pharmacist.

After his second glass of chardonnay, James told stories from his travels, making her smile and sigh and laugh as she put her napkin on the table and declared herself too full to move.

James had never enjoyed washing dishes so much, with Georgette's hysterical running commentary on the deep psychological meaning behind soap bubbles and dish sponges as background.

She waved him off when he offered to help her to the couch, giving her crutches a workout and assuring him it was like falling off a bicycle, that she could do laps with these things.

Then they sat on the couch and watched a Monty Python marathon. Georgette snickered at all the jokes, and James casually put his arm on the couch behind her, like a teen boy indecisive about whether his date would welcome his touch. Then she subtly shifted, and look at that, his arm was around her after all. And he felt a kind of peace he couldn't remember feeling in a long time.

The first time Georgette stifled a yawn, they both pretended it hadn't happened, as if that would mean this evening, this unspoken pact to forget their complicated past and just *be*, would be over. But the third time she stifled a yawn, James picked up the remote and flicked the TV off.

The mood changed.

Georgette grabbed her crutches. James let her. She clearly didn't want his help.

But two steps up the stairs, she was struggling, holding both crutches in one hand and the banister with the other.

He came up behind her. "You don't have to be a superhero."

"You've already done so much for me."

He gently tugged at the crutches.

She let him.

He tossed the crutches down the stairs, ignoring the clatter, and scooped her up. She wrapped her arms around his neck and leaned into his chest, and for a moment, he wished the guest bedroom was on the fiftieth floor of a skyscraper instead of one flight up and to the right.

Georgette sat on the twee comforter in the guest bedroom and tried to slow her heart rate and let her body cool off.

There had been a moment back there, as he'd kicked open the guest room door and set her down on the bed, a moment when he'd paused like he was about to join her. Her heart had jumped and her body went electric.

Lust was a tangible rope in the space between them. James took a step, and the space diminished. She made a sound in the back of her throat. Involuntary, mortifying. She wanted him. Wanted this.

He'd leaned in. She'd tilted her head up. An almost kiss.

She could already feel his heat against her, his taste and smell. And, after all, they'd kissed and fondled and were headed for more when his nephew had interrupted them. It was a done deal, a decision made. Now they could enjoy the consequences.

Consequences.

The look in his eyes as she'd left him on the rooftop at Roman's party, his demolished expression in the subway station. The charred photo of her on the fireplace surround.

If they made love tonight and then she left tomorrow, what would that mean? How could she risk her heart on a relationship with a man whose past she shared but didn't remember? With *this* man, who flirted with danger every time he went out on a shoot, who represented risk and the unknown?

And yet how could she not? The blood pulsing through her and the dark glow in his eyes made it inevitable. She gestured to the bed. "Do you—"

But the moment had passed. James was already heading toward the door. "Let me know if you need anything. I'll be right down the hall." And with that, he closed the door. She could hear his footsteps rapidly retreating back down the stairs.

She picked up her phone and texted the only person she knew who would get it.

Alanna was a risk taker. She'd had a series of secret sexual trysts with Miles before it had fallen apart in spectacular fashion.

*Etiquette question for the morally impaired: How did you know it was okay to sleep with Miles?*

The response came barely a minute later. Alanna must be hovering near her phone. Or playing Plants vs. Zombies. *You did it?!?!?!?!*

Georgette smiled at the phone, ignoring the ache in her chest. *Not yet. Trying to decide how stupid it would be if we did.*

The reply came quickly again. *Be stupid! It's more fun. It'll hurt later either way, so why not enjoy yourselves?*

*How do you keep your boundaries intact?*

Alanna's answer didn't help. *You don't.*

Georgette stared at the glowing light of her phone screen. So much for insight.

A final text from her friend: *He's hot! You like him! Go for it! Don't think so much!*

Not thinking was how Alanna got herself in trouble. It was emphatically not Georgette's style.

She turned the phone to vibrate and lay down, pulling the covers over herself. The pillowcase felt rough under her cheek. She closed her eyes, willing sleep.

The dream began mildly enough. Like most of the others, it started with James. A camera was secured to his chest, something bulky strapped to his back.

James on a rooftop. Head thrown back, laughing with a group of people.

James. Behind him, skyscrapers lit up the dark sky.

And then it changed. She'd dreamed this part before.

James. Plummeting off the side of the building. Falling.

Falling with him.

Darkness and wind and speed, sounds hollow echoes, wind roaring past. An improbably familiar rocky outcropping and churning water below, approaching fast, so fast, swirling rushing dizzying…

She woke up with a start, a whole-body jerk and grab—but it wasn't a pillow in her arms, it was a person.

And that brought her to full awareness.

"Shh. It was a dream." His voice was a whisper in the stillness.

"You came in. I didn't hear you."

"You were crying out." His breath tickled her ear. "Saying my name."

With his words, the dream came flooding back.

*James. Falling.*

She wrapped her arms around him, could feel his startled jerk. But she also felt his heart thumping against her ear, his slow deep breaths, his body heat, and was comforted. He was here. He was with her.

And she felt the changes signaling his body's response. His breathing got faster, rougher. His heartbeat hurried. Under the soft cotton of his sweatpants, his erection felt hard against her belly. He was turned on, and that knowledge set her aflame.

*Should* and *shouldn't* blew away, inconsequential bits of mental fluff. All that mattered was this. He was here. With her. Emphatically alive.

For once not analyzing, not measuring, not thinking about the consequences, she kissed him.

He responded instantly, and then they were wrapped in each other's arms, tongues and heat, and it was delicious, it was pulsing energy, it was everything. But it wasn't enough.

Feeling urgent, Georgette tugged at James's T-shirt. He sat up to slip it off over his head, then balled it up, tossed it across the room, and dove back into a deep kiss.

Her borrowed nightshirt next. She fumbled at the row of buttons—too many buttons—with shaking hands, her pounding pulse making it hard to focus on the tiny openings. James brushed her fingers aside and did it for her. In his haste, a button tore off.

"Sorry." The husky, breathless note in his voice sent a reckless shiver through her.

She grabbed the nightshirt with both hands and yanked it open. Buttons flew off, pinging around the room. "I'll buy another one for your sister." She let it drop away onto the bed.

"You did her a favor. It's hideous." James grinned, his eyes alight, which quickly slid to something reverent. "Look at you. You were beautiful at seventeen, but now you're…" He shook his head. "God."

She felt a laugh bubble up. "I'm just a woman. It's just a body."

"But it's *your* body." He leaned in, so close she could feel his breath hot on her throat, and slid his fingers across her nipples, which responded immediately. "I remember these. So perfect."

"I wish I could remember us. Like this."

"We never did end up in a bed. In my car, in the woods, under the bridge, but never in a bed. I lived for those moments. The way your body curved against mine. The weight of these in my hands." He laughed, deep in his throat, and kissed his way up her clavicle, licking her throat, keeping his hands on her breasts, playing with her nipples. Sensation spiraled through her, feeding off touch and words.

Oh God. She fell into the fire licking its way through her—it felt as if it had always been there, as if she'd burned for him, for this, her whole life. In a way, it was true. The almost-memory of being with him, the months-long tease of those dreams, the startling vividness of his presence in New York, and now this— sinking into his touch, his words, the stillness of the snowy silence, and the intensity of today. She slid her hands over his taut, muscular chest and he inhaled, clearly as hyperaware as she felt. Emboldened, she kept going, slipping her hand under the elastic of his sweatpants. She stroked his cock from root to tip.

He hissed against her ear. "If you keep doing that, I'll come like a teenager. No self-control."

She inhaled sharply, his arousal a heady turn-on. They were going to make love tonight. Now.

She slid her hand back up his cock, relishing the

smooth heat of him under her palm. "Did we ever make love?" *Were you my first?*

"God, you have no idea how much I wanted to." He slid his hands down her body, slipping one between her legs. "But no, we never went further than this." His fingers played against her center, and oh God, it felt so good.

"Did I say no? Was I shy and virginal? Did I make you crazy?" She could picture it, her younger self giggling and pulling away, scared of feeling too much.

"It wasn't just you. I was afraid I'd break you. You seemed so fragile, so lovely, and I..." If a shrug could convey wry amusement mixed with the height of sexual frustration, his did.

She squeezed his cock, and he nearly jumped off the bed. "You're big, but not *that* big." Then blushed in the dark. *Did I really say that?*

But he laughed. "Think you can take me on?" His turn to get flustered. "I mean—I didn't mean—" His hand at her crotch stilled, and he withdrew his fingers.

She slid her hand out from under his sweats. They stared at each other, silent in the dark, the tension pulsing between them. Questions unasked, emotions unanswered. His body tilted toward her, but he didn't make a move. It was up to her.

Now or never.

She hooked her thumbs into the waistband of his

sweats and yanked them down his legs, releasing his erection, then slid down the bed so she could take it in her mouth.

He threw his head back, his throat working, his body clenched with exquisite tension.

She licked up the underside of his cock, and he shivered in response.

"Yes."

"Yes?" His voice quivered, unsteady, and she felt a rush of power.

"Yes, I'm ready to take you on." She felt daring, wicked, utterly unlike herself as she stripped off her panties and let them drop to the braided rug, his sweats following soon after.

They were both naked now. His arousal jutted up, jaunty and bold, and his gaze devoured her, but he paused. "Are you certain? This changes things."

"Don't remind me."

But he wasn't in the mood for jokes. "Georgette."

"I'm certain." What had Alanna said? "I want to stop thinking so much. I want to feel. Will you help me feel?"

With a shaky inhale, he gathered her close. Skin to skin. Heartbeat to heartbeat. His erection pressed against her belly, and an answering, overpowering lust flared in her groin. A moment later, they were rolling on top of each other, kissing frantically, touching each other everywhere.

When he broke away to stroke down her body, she pulled him back. "No. Now." She scissored against him, needing the feel of his hardness and heat between her legs. *There. Yes. There.*

He slid into her, just the head, the merest tip, and she spasmed under him. Time was elastic, time folded over on itself, James was her lover, would be her lover, had been her lover, had never been. James was the man in her dreams, the man on her canvas, the man in her arms.

"Damn." He pulled out, pulled away.

She sat up. "What?" Oh God, not now. She'd kill him, that's what she'd do. "I know you, I—" She almost said *I love you,* but the thought led to an immediate clenching shot of fear. Did she? *Could* she? Her body throbbed for him. Was that love?

*Don't leave me in suspended animation. Don't do this.*

When he saw the look on her face, he turned back, briefly, and kissed her, a devouring, demolishing kiss. He murmured against her lips. "Bathroom. Condom."

"Oh…" It was an exhale. "Of course."

He came back a moment later, long enough for Georgette's all-body flush to subside, for her blood to return to something approaching normal, for the cool air to kiss her skin and make her acutely aware of the utter foreignness of this moment, this place. Even herself.

Had she ever had sex with someone before dating the guy at least two months? She'd even been known to put it on her calendar, schedule it after dinner and a concert—jazz or folk rock in a small local venue with a two-drink minimum. Sex with a man she knew but also didn't know, a man she wasn't officially involved with, a man she might never see again? Not like her.

James strode back into the room, magnificently naked, a condom covering his impressive erection, his sheer maleness startling in such a twee bedroom. He paused in the doorway when he saw that she'd draped herself in the comforter. "Having second thoughts?"

"Of course not." And yet a strange, unexpected fear rippled through her. She was hardly a virgin, but this would be different.

James could read emotional cues like the best psych student in her department. He sat on the bed beside her, his erection still poking up. He brushed her cheek with one finger, then let it drop away. "You can say no. I'll survive. I might have to go bury myself in a snow bank to cool off, but I'll survive."

She inhaled his scent, wood fire and pine forests, and God, he smelled so good. His momentary touch had set off sparks deep within her chest. And she wanted to say, *Take me. Fuck me. Be with me.* But she held back. "Aren't you a little scared too? Doesn't it—this—" She gestured between them. "Matter a little too much?"

Understanding dawned. "Because it's not just sex?"

"Because there's so much history between us." *So much I don't know.*

He caressed her bare thigh, tracing circles on her sensitive skin. "You may never remember, and if you do, I don't know how you'll feel, but I'm tired of saying no to something that feels so right. We're here. In it together. And I want to know what I've been missing. Don't you?"

His hand reached between her legs. Slowly, giving her plenty of time to pull away, to stop him.

She opened her legs to him. To his touch, then his tongue. Then, when she was ready, when they both were, to his cock.

He slid inside, and she nearly cried with the pleasure of it, the pureness of this hushed, perfect moment. She knew him, of course she did. She felt every inch of him, clenched her legs around him as he slid into her and she pushed up against him, the pressure-pleasure building, spreading from her core through her body, to her knees and toes, to her belly and her breasts, to her fingers and her throat. She kept her eyes open, looking up at him, and he gazed down at her as if he still couldn't believe what they were doing, as if the sight of her was as much pleasure as the feel.

They rolled over, and now he was beneath her on the sheets with their rows of acorns and bluebirds. She gazed down at him as she moved on top of him and he surged up into her. She watched his expressive mouth, his parted lips, his awed expression, and knew without any hesitation, without any doubt, that he *knew* her. Yes, he was inside her, filling her up, and the movements of his hips, his cock, the slap and pull was pure pleasure—but it wasn't just his body, it was him. James. Her first love.

And then she stopped thinking, became incapable of thought, as he flipped them around again, knelt over her, driving into her, harder now, more focused, his expression strained, holding back, but barely. And she felt it, the exquisite sexual tension spiraling, building to a crescendo—and wham, she was there, with an involuntary exclamation as spasm after spasm rolled through her, clench and release, joy and repletion. James's face was a mask of pleasure-pain as he responded to her climax. One more thrust, then he too gasped and shouted his ecstatic release.

He buried his face in her neck. "God. Georgette. God."

She hummed with pleasure. "I know."

A quick hug, then he rolled off her, disposed of

the condom, and rolled back to gather her in close. He nuzzled her hair. "You are magnificent."

"You are."

"No, you." She could hear the smile in his voice. Her bare legs were getting chilled and his body felt heavy against hers, but she never wanted to let go.

# Chapter Seventeen

When Georgette woke up, stretching luxuriously, feeling the satisfying ache of a delicious morning after, she rolled over toward James—and found an empty space in the bed. He'd been there all night, his arm protectively curved around her, his body tucked against hers. She'd slept more soundly than she had in years, in dreamless peace and comfort.

This morning, the sky was clear blue, snow kept falling off the roof in gentle thuds, and James was gone.

He'd left the crutches by the bed, as well as a smooth tree branch with the twigs whittled off and a decorative purple ribbon tied around the middle.

She picked it up. It felt damp and cool. Freshly cut. A gift, clearly. Not exactly flowers, was it? Then again, it was midwinter, and they were presumably still trapped up here.

Still, an odd gift.

*Oh, wait.*

She leaned, hard. It held her weight. Could she…?

Carefully, slowly, she stood.

Yes. She could. Forget the crutches. She could walk.

James had made her a cane.

She got dressed and went downstairs. James wasn't there either, but he'd left coffee in the coffeemaker and a toasted muffin on the kitchen counter. Outside, she could hear the distinctive sounds of shoveling. Determined James, ready to break them out of here.

The thought was strangely painful. When the road cleared, she'd have to go. Back to real life, three hundred miles south of here. Which was how it had to be. He wasn't part of her life. She couldn't let herself get entangled with someone like him. Never mind their history, he was a dangerous man to love. A reckless man.

As she poured herself a cup of coffee, Georgette glanced at the photos on the wall behind the couch and shivered.

No. This wasn't real life. Not her life. This was a magical interlude, but when it was over, it was over. That's how it had to be. As her mother might say, "Better to lead with the head than the heart, it gets you in less trouble."

It had always sounded so easy. Until now.

James unzipped his winter jacket, but sweat still dripped down the back of his neck in rivulets. He unwrapped his scarf and tossed it aside, letting his knit cap follow. The cold air was a relief, and he dug back into the snow, which was already crusting over a day into the storm aftermath. He'd cleared most of the driveway. If they needed to, they could probably get out. If the road was clear.

That was, if he was willing to let her go. After last night, he wasn't sure he'd ever let her go again.

Assuming she gave him a choice. True, she'd been open to him last night in her post-dream vulnerability, but what would she be like now? Their lovemaking had been one of the most powerful experiences of his life, and he could tell it had been the same for her. But knowing Georgette, she'd already begun to put it in a box in her mind and put that box inside another box, tied with strings attached, lashed around with *it didn't mean anything after all* justifications, ready to stick in the back of a closet to be forgotten and only looked at on special occasions or when it was convenient.

Or hey, maybe he was underestimating her. Maybe she was ready to move to Pine Mountain, live with him, and eventually get married and live happily ever after.

He chuckled aloud at that. The woman had stuffed her memories of him so far back in her mind, she didn't even know how to retrieve them, and she was going to toss her entire life over after one night in bed with him? He was good, but he wasn't a sex god.

He bent to his work. Better to be a realist like Georgette. Better to clear the driveway so he could be ready when she took it in her head that she had to leave *right now, not one second later.* Better to prepare his heart for her inevitable departure.

Something hard and cold smacked the back of his neck. He whirled around.

Georgette stood by the cabin door, leaning on the stick he'd left her. Laughing. "Gotcha!" She scooped up another hunk of snow.

James merely shook his head, scattering the snow from his hair, and grinned. "Like that, is it?" He grabbed a huge handful of snow and tossed it in her direction. It fell apart midair, a mini snowstorm.

While he was scooping up more snow, Georgette tossed a fully formed ball at him, hitting him right in the chest.

"Oof! I'll get you for that!" But he was grinning wider than she'd seen him yet, smiling like his face was going to crack wide open. This open delight, this mischievous, carefree boy—this was the real James.

He rushed forward, let loose with both hands, and buried her in a shower of snow.

Snow in her mouth, snow on her cheeks, burning cold and bright. She too laughed, blinking away the melting flakes, licking cold drops off her lips. It tasted sharp and clean.

She met James's gaze. His eyes were narrowed

against the icy glare and dark with desire. Heat flared, hovering in the air between them, which had turned thick with intent.

He kissed her. His lips were warm in the cold air, his tongue testing, twining, sliding against hers. His body close, his scent...

She closed her eyes and breathed in the smell of him, the taste of him, dizzy with longing. Longing and something else.

*Kissing James, but a younger version, his dark hair untrimmed and falling over his face, his face narrower, his eyes lit with an unholy delight. His unzipped down jacket brushed against hers; they were two roly-poly winter bears. Snow fell around them, cold sparks on her cheeks, contrasting sharply with his hot hands sliding up under her layers of shirt and sweater. A voice called from a rickety old porch: "James! Get your ass in here! Stop feeling up your tootsie!" James laughed against her mouth. A giddy feeling, bubbles in her throat, teen love transcendent.*

Kissing Georgette was the only thing he'd ever done, the only thing he ever wanted to do. He could drown in her sweet taste, sink into her luscious feminine curves, and never come up for air, a happy death. Ice on the driveway, cold dry air, a sharp wind —none of it mattered, none of it was important. He was kissing Georgette, and it wasn't just a middle-of-the-night vulnerability. They were doing this with full intent, with the burn of the ice and snow and sun, the clarity of daylight. It could be minus ten degrees right now and he wouldn't know it. His body was a conflagration.

Then she pulled back, just a hair, but enough. He opened his eyes to find her staring at him in glazed bemusement.

"I know you," Georgette whispered. "I remember us."

He almost laughed. She'd stopped kissing him to tell him this? But then he realized what it meant. "You remember?"

"Standing outside your house. Kissing. Snow was falling. Your jacket was burnt orange, and you had a bright blue scarf. Your hair fell over your eyes." She touched his hair wonderingly. "Your father was calling you in. I remember that. He didn't sound pleased. He called me a tootsie."

James laughed, a hiccup, his breath caught in the middle. His father had been dead for five years, and the thought of him still hurt at odd moments. "Sounds like him."

"You don't remember? Maybe you have amnesia. You should look into that."

"Good thing I have a professional shrink close at

hand."

"I don't know. You're a tricky case. I'd have to know more about your situation before I could agree to take you on." Her voice was teasing, her gaze warm.

"Well, Madame Headshrinker, I seem to have a problem with my high school girlfriend."

Her gaze turned wary.

"She fights dirty in a snowball fight. What do you think that's about? Does she feel like she's not my equal? She's such a puny little thing, maybe I'm too much man for her."

Georgette gasped in mock indignation and scooped up a hunk of snow. It shed flakes as she brought it up to his chest, threatening his open-collared shirt. "Think carefully, Falk. You might find yourself out in the cold."

He grabbed her and pulled her close. "I dare you."

Her quick inhale, her dilated irises showed she was as turned on as he was, but she rubbed a handful of snow against his clavicle anyway.

He gasped at the sudden cold. "Oh no, you don't." He crushed her against him and kissed her again, his tongue thrusting into her mouth, a mimic of the real thing, the act of lovemaking, and why not?

Georgette kissed him back, full force, not holding back. When she put her hands up to his cheeks, her touch burned with snow-dusted cold, and he loved it.

At the same time, he knew—with far too much clarity
—that, for her, it was snowbound lust. She'd run off as
soon as the roads cleared. On the long distance bus,
she'd probably make a list: *Why I Shouldn't Stay with
James.* This kiss was a snapshot of a winter moment,
already fading at the edges.

He wanted to grab on, hold her tight. Wanted to
do something reckless and stupid. Run naked into the
snow. Climb a skyscraper with a grappling hook and
his bare hands. Jump out of an airplane into a
snowbank and clamber out, blind and frozen and alive.
Make love to Georgette until he'd imprinted her skin
with his scent, with his body, with his entire being.

And so he kissed her, rough, and relished her
moan, and the way she braced herself against him, but
it wasn't enough. If this was all they had, if this was the
only time together, it had to count more. He craved
adventure, exhilaration.

He gathered her into his arms and carried her to a
huge snowbank. She flung her arms around him and
shrieked when he sank into the snow mound with her,
the force of their landing breaking the outer coating of
last night's frost.

As they fell into the mass of softness layered on
softness, he kissed her, openmouthed, relishing the
cold air and hot breath, and slid his hand under her
borrowed sweater, relieved to find no bra, just pebbled

nipples so tight against his palms. He cupped her ass and pulled her toward him, rubbing her against his erection, making his intention clear. The snow beneath them compacted and hardened into shape, and he slipped her—no, his—sweatpants down her legs.

Georgette jerked back at the feel of the snow against her bare legs. "You're crazy, you know that?" But she said it against his mouth, smiling. Behind them, his front door was still open, wafting warm air out into the hushed snowscape.

"Crazy is one of my better traits." He removed his coat and slipped it under her legs. After all, he didn't need it. He was immune to the cold. It didn't stand a chance against the fire raging inside him. He slipped the condom out of his back pocket—he'd put it there this morning in a fantasy that involved the living room rug and a roaring fire, but this was better.

Georgette climbed on top of him, pulling his sweater up and kissing his chest, licking his nipples, a wild gleam in her eyes. She was in this too, right here with him, and the thought was as intoxicating as the feel of her body against his, the anticipation of what they were about to do.

She unzipped his pants, pulled his cock out—the cold a shock of the most erotic sort, ice and fire—and then she took the condom from his hand. When she unwrapped it over him, he was harder than he'd ever

been. He lay back as she straddled him on the
snowbank, her winter coat open around her, her shirt
hiked up to reveal smooth belly sloping down to her
mons and her bare, beautiful hips and groin. And then
—*then*—she slid onto him, sheathing him in her
unbelievable tight heat, and he was a goner. She rode
him, sliding down as he pushed up, her breath
catching, her eyes wide, alight. Laughing with
wonderment. "This is crazy." Her voice was thick with
desire. "Crazy amazing."

A wind kicked up. She clenched around him, and
it was, if anything, even more exciting. He grabbed the
edges of her coat and wrapped it close around the two
of them, a cocoon, sexy and dark, but the snow was all
around them, an icy bed to their lovemaking, his down
jacket a thin layer between them and the ice, and they
both shivered as they moved against and with each
other.

"Do you want to go inside?" *Say no.*

"Yes. No." She slid down onto him again. "Fuck
me, James. Fuck me fast before I turn into an icicle.
Warm me up."

He rolled them over. Now he was above her, their
faces inches apart, and he did what she wanted. He
drove into her, fast and faster, hard and harder, again
and again. A snowflake got caught on his cheek, he
could see the glitter of her wet lashes and the flakes in

her hair, and he thought if he died right now, it would be a perfect end. Her tight responsiveness drove him wild. His Georgette, this moment, entirely with him, engulfing and surrounding him, her heart pounding in chaotic rhythm with his, the best adrenaline rush of them all.

As he felt her about to come—that telltale tightness, the momentary pause before the rush—he grabbed a handful of snow and sprinkled it on her breasts. She gasped and came and came and came, delicious spasms tightening around him. Her eyes dilated in pleasure as she locked gazes with him. And it was too much, so intense—he climaxed, a full body spasm. No thought, no wistful memories, no wishes for the future, just pure sensation, purely in the present, the freezing cold, utterly hot, delicious present moment.

They laughed as they scrambled up, still heated from within in the aftermath, desperate to get inside before their bodies cooled down. James carried Georgette into the house, leaving the snow-coated sweatpants behind. When they got inside, he brushed the glimmering snow out of her hair and off her bare thighs and kissed her and laughed again with her laughter at what they'd just done.

But his throat felt tight, like he might cry. It had been so perfect—so daring and wild and perfect—and it would never be like that again. Not with her, therefore not with anyone. Because Georgette wasn't his, not really. They'd been playing make-believe, pretending this was lasting and real. But the snow was melting, and this idyll would be over the moment she walked out the door. She wouldn't stay in his life. She wasn't ready to give him her full trust, let alone her heart.

# Chapter Eighteen

Georgette leaned heavily on James for support as they entered the drafty old farmhouse, wielding the branch cane with her other hand. Maybe she could whack James's mother with it if she got nasty again. Her ankle throbbed from the unaccustomed walking, even though James had carried her halfway across the expanse between his home and his mother's. His clean woodsy smell lingered on her skin. Or maybe that was from earlier. She flushed, hot with the memory.

As James hung up their coats, she paused, eyeing the layer of coats on the rack as she heard the rumble of conversation beyond the foyer threshold. "I thought it was a small family gathering. How did everyone else get here? Snowmobiles? Helicopters?"

James gave her his arm, and they walked into the living room. "Didn't I mention that the road to town was cleared this morning?"

"Oddly, no, I don't think you did. Guess it slipped your mind."

He gave her a wicked little-boy-caught grin. "I was distracted."

"But if the roads are clear, we need to figure out —"

He interrupted her, talking over her. "I know, but

I think we should—"

A familiar-looking woman their age rushed over. Her long black hair flared as she hurried across the living room. "Georgette? It *is* you! I heard a rumor, but I didn't believe it!" She embraced Georgette, enveloping her in a cloud of jasmine and clove.

"Teresa?" Georgette gripped James's arm harder to avoid toppling over. He held his hand under her elbow, steadying her.

Her old friend pulled away to give her a once-over. "You have to ask? Of course it's me!"

"It's just—it's been a while, you know?" The scrawny fifteen-year-old was now a full-blown woman, complete with curves and shiny hair—and a sweet pregnancy bulge. The huge ear-to-ear grin, though, that was the same.

Teresa took in Georgette's hand on James's sleeve. "So you two are..." She gestured. "I'm so glad. You were the best thing that happened to him."

Beside her, James tensed. "Teresa, I love you like a sister, but shut up."

A woman waltzed over and gave Teresa a wink before popping a mini hot dog in her mouth. "So you know, that actually *is* how he talks to his sisters." One of his sisters, then. Willa or Karen? James had briefed her on the way over. Willa was the middle child, recently married. This woman was at least ten years older than James. She must be Karen, Chester's mother. Had they ever met?

Karen gave Georgette a sideways look. "And you are…?" But the way she said it sounded like a lie.

"Karen." James's tone was a warning. "You remember Georgette."

"Right. Of course." Karen flashed Georgette an insincere smile. "Didn't recognize you. It's been so long."

Teresa snagged Georgette's elbow. "Come on. Let's find somewhere to talk. We have so much catching up to do!"

As she went off with Teresa, leaning on the cane but trying not to be conspicuous about it, Georgette heard James lean in toward his sister. "We need to talk. You can't do that."

"Do what?" His sister sounded so innocent.

"You know damned well what." His muttered voice fell off as Georgette went out of range, but she'd heard enough. He had her back, and it felt surprisingly warming.

Beside her, Teresa gave Georgette one of her thousand-watt smiles. "The guy's crazy about you. Always has been." She pointed to the nearby staircase. "This okay? Or should I claim pregnant priority and kick those lollygaggers off the couch?" A group of elderly women had crowded onto the sofa and armchair, and were drinking and laughing.

"I'd hate to break up the fun. Stairs is fine. And closer."

Georgette gratefully settled onto a wide, carpeted step and stretched out her leg, resting it on a lower step.

Teresa sat with care, leaning back to balance the beach-ball-sized lump under her high waistline. "I'm glad you're back together."

"It's more complicated than that."

"So I hear. You blanked on the entire relationship, huh?"

"He told you?"

"His mom told Fred Streeter. Our old history teacher? He's principal now, and my boss."

"You're at the high school?"

"Yup. Biology teacher." Teresa patted her protruding belly. "My students claim I'm their lab study. They pore over every ultrasound picture and have been reading along in *What to Expect When You're Expecting*. Maybe next semester I should teach chemistry and bring in baby spit-up for them to experiment on. And you? You're a shrink, I hear? Good for you! Do you love it?"

"Still getting my degree, but I like it so far."

"You always were good at getting inside people's heads."

"Everyone's except my own, it seems."

"That's always the hardest."

Georgette put her hand on her old friend's shoulder. "I'm sorry I was such a flake. Disappearing like that all these years. I miss you."

"I miss you too." Teresa leaned in for a hug.

A sound emanated from upstairs, like someone choking or coughing. Georgette glanced at Teresa, who clearly heard it too, and grabbed the banister to pull herself up to a stand. The sound came again, clearer this time. A curse, in a young male voice still in the wobble of puberty.

"Should we?" Georgette gestured up the stairs.

"You think?"

A curse, then the smack of something lobbed against a wall.

"We can always leave if he doesn't want company."

With the rail and Teresa's arm for support, going upstairs was reasonably quick and only somewhat clumsy.

Georgette knocked on the bedroom door.

"Go away!"

"Do you know Chester?" Georgette whispered to Teresa, who shook her head.

*Okay, then.* "Chester, it's Georgette. We met yesterday at your Uncle James's. You invited me to come today. Well, your grandmother did, but you conveyed the message while gazing up at James's admittedly intriguing ceiling."

A choked laugh. "Come in. If you have to."

Georgette opened the door. Teresa gave her a pat on the back and then stepped away.

She went inside.

Chester was lying on the bed, on top of the covers, clutching a pillow to his chest. The detritus of his angst attack lay around him: tossed books, papers, clothing. "Did my mother send you?"

"Your mother's Karen, right? I don't think she likes me." She sat on the end of the bed, resting her cane against her leg.

"She doesn't. She said you must be lying. Said that nobody outside the daytime soaps has amnesia, so obviously you're toying with her brother's emotions and that's totally messed up. Only she used more colorful language." He rolled over and looked at her. "I probably shouldn't tell you all that, huh?"

"Not that I couldn't guess. Can't blame her, it's pretty far-fetched." Even so, the criticism hurt more than it should. "So you want to tell me what's going on? I'm pretty sure you're not heartbroken over my love life."

"Are you in love with him?" He tossed the pillow toward the armchair on the other side of the room. It landed neatly on the seat.

"Good aim." No way was she going to answer that particular question.

"So you are." Chester gave her a sly glance.

Georgette laughed, startled. "Ever think of becoming a therapist? You're sharper than most of my colleagues."

"I'm going to be a hockey player. Only I'm not if I don't get out of here. SUNY Plattsburgh won't want a B student who sat out the biggest game of the season."

"Plattsburgh, huh? They have a good team. You aiming for the Olympics?"

He plucked at the seams of the obviously handmade quilt. "Yeah, maybe. Dunno."

"I hear the roads are cleared now. You can probably head home tomorrow. Will that be soon enough to play the big game?"

"Probably. If Coach hasn't put someone else in already." But he didn't seem to be cheered by the thought.

*Hmm.* "Is there a girl? Or a boy?"

He flushed. "No!" Then he met her gaze. "Yeah. My moms don't know. I didn't want to tell them, in case it didn't turn into anything. But we were supposed to go out tonight. There's this big New Year's party at Brandon's, he's our goalie. It took me five months to ask her out—five *months*—and when I did, she laughed and said what took me so long? And she said I play hockey like a rock star, all guts and smarts. Nobody's ever said anything like that to me before. It's tonight, the party. *Tonight.* Meanwhile, I'm stuck here, in backwards Pine Miserable Excuse for a Mountain, where they don't plow the roads and it snows all the time. Even though the roads are clear enough to drive, my mom Gretchen says she doesn't want to risk it. Alexia is never going to speak to me again. And I was going to kiss her and everything, at midnight, you know? Only now I won't be there and she'll probably make out with Brandon. I would. He's cuter than me."

Had she been this passionate, this all-or-nothing as a teenager? Hard to imagine. James must have been. She could see him like this—the torrent of words, the giddiness and terror, the feeling that love was so fragile, it could fall apart in a second. "Have you texted her? Let her know what happened?"

"She didn't write back."

*Hmm.*

Then again, he *was* a teen boy. "What did you say?"

He handed her his phone, then grabbed a second pillow and tossed it at the wall. It fell back onto the bed.

Georgette scrolled through. He'd written, *Not gonna make it tonite.*

"Of course she didn't write back."

"What? Why?" He grabbed the pillow and squeezed it hard.

"She said you were a rock star and you say *not gonna make it?* She's feeling pretty vulnerable right now. Tell her how you feel. Give her something more, let her know you care. Girls need that." *Everyone needs that.*

*James needs that.*

She should tell him how she felt about him. She could say, *"I think I might be falling for you, and it terrifies me."* Or *"I'll never be able to get you out of my head after this week. I've never felt like this before."*

Even thinking the words made her squirm. "On second thought, don't. I mean, if it feels too hard."

As if conjured, James appeared in the doorway. "I've been looking for you everywhere." He proffered her phone. "Your phone kept ringing. It was in your coat pocket. I had to answer it. Someone named Trudy?"

Georgette grabbed the phone. "Trudy? Everything okay?"

"I'm in the bathroom. I kind of, I tried, I thought about, I took…"

"Okay, take a deep breath and start again. One thought at a time. I'm here. I'm listening."

Georgette stood up. James immediately offered his arm for support. She leaned on it as she walked out of

Chester's room and into the upstairs hallway. Chester picked up his own phone and stared down at it, frowning as if he expected it to start arguing with him. Then, slowly, he pecked out a message.

Meanwhile, on the phone, Trudy burst into tears. "I'm holding the pills. In my hand. I took two, and then I...I don't know, I don't—I think I want to, but I don't know!" Her wail broke Georgette's heart.

As James started to help her down the stairwell, Georgette halted, squeezing his bicep so hard, he could feel the bruises. "Trudy, put the pills down. You can't feel better if you're dead. Yes, I know how it feels. I do. But the fact that you called me means you don't really want to go through with it. Trust your gut on this. It knows, even if you don't, that you're stronger than this. Stronger than him."

*Oh. Oh wow.*

James led Georgette into his mother's small study and settled her in the old-fashioned wooden chair, then got a stool and raised her foot up while she was talking. She nodded at him in thanks.

"It'll be okay. I promise. I'll stay on the phone as long as you need me. Would you consider—would you go to the hospital if I set things up on my end? You wouldn't have to go to the emergency room, I'm pretty sure I can arrange that from here..."

The female voice on the other end said something anguished, trailing tears.

"I would if I could, I swear. I want to be there. But I'm upstate, and the weather is bad. Do you know how to reach your parents?"

Parents? Yes, the voice had been that young. His heart broke for Georgette's client, and for Georgette.

Georgette continued. "No, I understand. We'll deal with them later. I can call my friend Jeanine. She's great. We work together. You'll like her, I promise."

The voice on the other end sounded distrustful.

He cleared his throat. "Georgette."

She waved him off.

"If you need—"

She turned away, resolutely ignoring him, sounding so steady, so rock solid on the phone. "Okay. Breathe. Walk me through what happened. Back before that. How did you feel when you woke up this morning? No, it's okay. I've got all the time in the world."

He grabbed a pencil, scribbled a note on the margin of a handy utility bill, and handed it to her.

She waved it off, but he pointed to the paper. *Read it.*

When she did, her eyebrows shot up. *Really?* She mouthed the word.

He nodded. *Really.*

She inhaled sharply—relief and worry both, he was guessing—then spoke into the phone. "What if I could be there in four hours?" She glanced out the window. "Maybe five."

There was an audible exhale, then tears and more words.

"Of course. I said it and I meant it. But I'd like to get you somewhere safe until I arrive. Is that okay? Good, yes. I'll call my friend now, and she can— No, no, I understand. I can stay on the phone. I can talk to you as long as you need." She rubbed her forehead and gave James a helpless look.

James whispered, "Let me talk to her." In truth, he had no idea if he was up to the task. But if this girl was suicidal and alone on New Year's Eve, then she needed to hear a voice on the phone. And Georgette had other phone calls to make if she was going to get this girl the help she needed.

After a momentary hesitation, she nodded her agreement and told the girl on the phone, "You know what? I have a great idea. I'm here with my friend James. He's been through a lot in his life. He was suicidal once too."

James raised his eyebrows at her. She gestured, *Go with it.*

"So he gets it, yeah. And you know, the guy's perspective might help, am I right?"

The voice on the other end sounded dubious at best. Rightfully so. Why had he offered?

Because he had to. Which didn't make it easier. When Georgette handed him her phone, he fumbled and nearly dropped it. What on earth could he say to a city kid, a brokenhearted girl on the verge of the unthinkable?

And then he knew exactly what to say. Of course he knew. He put the phone to his ear. "Hi, Trudy, right? I'm James. I do know something of what you're going through." He handed Georgette his phone and moved a few feet away to give them both a small measure of privacy.

She nodded at him approvingly as she dialed a number and spoke into his phone, her voice hushed.

He continued, "I was crazy in love with a girl in high school, and when she—" Better if he skipped the part about how he'd watched helplessly as she fell into a ravine. "When she left me, I couldn't function. I lost twenty pounds in two weeks. When school started, I couldn't make myself go."

Georgette gave him a wide-eyed look. He grimaced, but it couldn't be helped. This girl needed truth. She needed pain. His pain. And if that meant Georgette had to hear how fucked-up he'd been over her, so be it.

Trudy made an agreeing sound. "You couldn't go

to school because you'd see her there, right? That's me. It hurts so much when I see Elias with Vanessa, and I swear he waits to put his tongue down her throat until I'm standing right in front of them. Like he gets off on my pain." The girl's voice was thready but alert. Involved.

"I escaped that particular hell. She wasn't at school. She'd—uh, she changed schools."

"To get away from you? Hard core. Elias hasn't done that. Yet."

"Thing is, it doesn't matter. When you've been with someone you're crazy about and they're gone but you're still there, you see them everywhere."

"Yeah. Every-fucking-where. Like the memories are lying in wait, ready to jump me."

"Exactly. So I started skipping school. Which worked until my father found out. That didn't go over so well."

"But you—Ms. Soren said you tried to off yourself?"

Georgette hadn't known. She'd been giving Trudy a line, some reason to trust him. But it was the truth. "Yeah. Once. I was driving down a dark mountain road in the rain and I thought, *it'll look like an accident. My parents won't know.* So I gunned the motor and steered off the road, aiming toward a steep cliff."

When had this become about him and his own personal hell? But he felt a strange kinship with this kid, so he kept talking.

Georgette had hung up with her caller. She nodded at him. She'd gotten someone to help. Good.

On the phone, Trudy's voice was hushed. "What happened?"

He laughed dryly. "Someone was watching out for me that night, I guess. I lost control of the wheel, the car skidded out and hit a tree I hadn't even seen. It flipped over, and I landed upside down, hanging by my seat belt, five inches from the edge of eternity."

Georgette sat in his mother's hard-backed office chair, his phone in her lap, staring at him. He nodded at her. Now she knew. So there was that.

But Trudy was waiting on the other line. So he went on, talking both to her and to Georgette. "That's how I know you'll be okay. I was. After that, I was. Sometimes you have to go to the edge of the cliff and look down to know you'll make it."

Trudy's voice was hushed. "Thank you, Mr.—"

"You can call me James."

"Thank you, James."

# Chapter Nineteen

Hospital chairs sucked. All angles and edges, no ergonomic anything. On the other side of the room, beyond the curtain, a child snored lightly in a hospital bed while her mother slumbered in an armchair that unfolded to become a single bed. Probably uncomfortable too, but at least you could be horizontal.

Thing was, he couldn't ask for one. Because he shouldn't be here. Georgette could be, as a stand-in for Trudy's admitting physician or some such—James hadn't been listening too closely when she'd called her supervising professor to talk through the logistics—but he should be in a hotel room right now, ordering room service and a stiff drink after that hellish drive down here. He wasn't kin, and he wasn't any kind of doctor or psychological wizard or anything remotely close to official. But after the vividly beautiful Jeanine had conferred with Georgette and the quiet, shy Susannah had given Trudy a good-bye hug, the two of them had left, back to their separate New Year's celebrations. He couldn't leave Georgette alone here all night, could he?

Okay, he could have. But he didn't want to. He wanted every moment with her he could get. Wanted to carry the tenuous bond they'd forged during their cabin idyll a few hours into the future, because he had a feeling that was all they'd have. Georgette was risk averse, and falling in love was a hell of a risk. As for him? He was already in too deep. From the moment he saw her face, pale behind the scratched-up bus window, he'd been irrevocably tied to her. He was here for as long as she'd have him.

He shifted in his seat yet again, stretched out his legs, rotated his shoulders, and massaged his neck. Where was Georgette with that coffee?

"You're still here." Trudy sleepily blinked at him. "What's your name again?"

"James."

"The one I talked to on the phone."

"The very one."

"Are you and Ms. Soren boyfriend and girlfriend?"

"I was wondering the same thing." He grinned.

Trudy nodded, somber. "Are my parents coming?"

"I think so. We should ask Georgette—Ms. Soren. She'll have the latest."

"Where is she?"

"Getting coffee. Please tell me you don't drink it."

Trudy rolled her eyes at him. "I'm sixteen, not six. I drink coffee."

"Forgive me." He stretched his arms over his head, trying to unkink the muscles in his upper back.

"Did you get over her?"

*Georgette.* A vision of her oval face, her eyes glazed with lust as she rode him on the snow mound earlier today. "Get over who?"

"The girl you were obsessed with. The one who made you—you know. Drive off the road."

"Right. Of course." Get over her? He never had. But to say that to this fragile young girl? "After a while, it mattered less. I thought about her less. She became less real to me, you could say. You'll get there. It's a kind of healing process, only from the inside instead of on the skin."

Georgette came into the room, carrying a tray with three thick paper cups. She still leaned on the makeshift birch branch cane, but less heavily. She was healing too. "You'll definitely get there. After a while, you'll forget the intensity of your feelings for Elias. It'll be like a dream you once had." She glanced at James, blinking hard, then smiled at Trudy. "I got you hot chocolate, I hope you don't mind. If you prefer coffee, I'll drink the chocolate."

Trudy reached her hand out. "Chocolate, please."

Georgette handed James a coffee, then pulled up her chair and sat by Trudy's bed and peeled the lid off her own. The two of them talked in low voices.

James felt like an eavesdropper, like he shouldn't be here. He got up, setting his cup down. "I'm going for a walk around the floor. Stretch my legs."

Georgette nodded at him, then went back to talking with the girl. Her look warmed him more than the hot liquid had.

He paced the hall with rapid strides, seeking to clear his overactive mind. Until an orderly gave him a reproving glare. "Children are sleeping," she said in a lilting Jamaican accent. After that, he walked more slowly. Not nearly as satisfying.

What a way to spend New Year's Eve. Speaking of which...

At ten minutes to midnight, he stopped at the vending machine, dug out some change, and bought three miniature bottles of apple juice. Then he went back to be with Georgette.

As he pulled back the curtain around Trudy's side of the room, Georgette put her finger to her lips. The girl was asleep.

"It's almost midnight," he whispered, and gestured toward Georgette with one of the apple juice bottles. "A toast?"

She stood, leaning on the cane. "Looks like it's just us." The little girl and her mom were fast asleep on the other side of the room.

He helped her over to the wide window ledge, where they sat next to each other, twisting off their bottle caps in unison.

"Not the way you expected to spend tonight, is

it?"

"Small cost for saving someone's life." He glanced over at the slumbering teen. "But she's safe here. Can't you go back to your apartment now?"

She cradled the drink between her palms. "I need to talk to her parents. Make sure they understand what happened. And why." She sounded grim.

"They're coming, then?"

"I talked to her mother on the phone again half an hour ago. They're taking a night train. They're on it right now."

"So they're open to hearing it."

"I think so. Finally." She looked over at the shadowed figure on the bed. "Poor kid."

"You're good with her."

"I've always felt an affinity for teenagers. The confusion, the angst." She glanced at him. "And now you're going to say I don't remember, so how can I relate? But I do. Somehow, I do."

"Maybe part of you has always remembered."

"Maybe so."

He could hear faint whoops from the street. A TV down the hall echoed a cheer. The clock on the wall confirmed it. Midnight.

James raised his plastic apple juice bottle. "Happy New Year."

She tilted her bottle to silently clink with his.

"Happy New Year. Whatever happens next, I'm glad this year brought you into my life." She drank a sip and made a face. "Corn syrup and artificial flavoring."

"Let's get a bottle of Dom tomorrow and usher in the new year in style."

She grinned. "Let me guess. Snowbank or fur rug?"

He scoffed. "This is the city. Rooftop."

A shadow crossed her face. "Of course." She chugged the rest of the bottle, leaving James wondering what he'd said to break the mood.

"But a hotel room will do in a pinch."

"How about my—I mean Alanna's—apartment? She's in Vermont with Miles. She's got a queen-size bed."

Trudy's sleepy voice came from the hospital bed. "I *thought* you guys were doing it."

James exchanged embarrassed glances with Georgette. "Nailed us."

"You mean you nailed her." The teenager giggled at her own humor. She must be feeling better. Suicidal people didn't usually make silly jokes, did they?

James woke slowly, then abruptly, like swimming up from the bottom of a pool, holding his breath, and then making a go for it before he started gasping water. It might have had something to do with the blonde woman standing at the foot of the bed, staring at their naked tangled limbs. He pulled the comforter up to cover them, and Georgette blinked awake.

"Who the hell are you?" The blonde frowned at him, darkly foreboding. Well, as darkly foreboding as a petite barefoot woman could be. "Georgie, I thought you were in that Adirondack town with—oh." Her eyebrows shot up. "You're him."

He sat up, clutching the coverlet. "James Falk, at your service." This must be Alanna, Georgette's host.

Georgette raised herself to her elbows. "Sorry to take over your bed. I'll change the sheets, I promise. I thought you were staying in Vermont through the weekend."

"S'okay." Alanna rubbed her calf with her other foot, standing on one foot to do so. "I got bored, so I came back."

"Without Miles?" Georgette fished on the floor for her clothes, came up with James's T-shirt instead. He nodded at her, bemused by the women's exchange.

"Without Miles." Alanna flopped on the end of the bed and stared at James. "So you're him. Wow. Georgette was like a woman obsessed when she was painting you. I've never seen her like that. Ms. Cool, Calm, and Collected was a nervous wreck."

Georgette was half-obscured by his shirt. She pulled it over her head and reemerged. "Alanna."

"What? It's true." Alanna gave her friend an innocent glance, then turned back to James. "You must be pretty special."

James grinned. "That I am."

"James." Georgette gave him an admonishing look.

He grabbed her and gave her a kiss. "That's the real reason you forgot me. I was too much for you."

"That must be it." She pushed him away and stood up, reaching for her walking stick. "Alanna, we'll be out of your hair in an hour, I swear. Sorry about this."

Alanna gave an airy wave. "Don't hurry on my account. This is so much more interesting than listening to Miles's parents discuss the intricacies of Vermont politics yet again."

Georgette sat back down and put her arm around her friend. James used the opportunity to rescue his pants and put them on.

"Are you breaking up with Miles?" Georgette's voice was soft but matter-of-fact, a you-can-tell-me tone he was starting to recognize as her therapist mode.

"No! Of course not." Alanna yanked the ends of her hair. "I hope not."

James frowned. "I think I should get going. This sounds like girl talk."

Alanna waved at him. "Help yourself to lunch."

She glanced at Georgette, sly. "You guys must have been partying hard last night. It's noon already."

He smothered a laugh. "Party animals, that's us. Lukewarm apple juice and all."

Georgette gave him a half smile, but her eyes were gleaming with something that, if he didn't know better, looked like love. Tenderness, anyway.

Alanna glanced between them with raised eyebrows. "I'm sensing a story here."

"And I'm sensing a woman avoiding the issue," Georgette retorted. "You're seriously going to break up with Miles because you don't want to move into his apartment? Are you afraid he's going to fall out of love with you once he discovers you mix the darks in with the lights when you do laundry? He's not your father, Alanna. He's madly in love with you. I thought you loved him too."

Man, his woman was good. She could see right into the heart of it. With everyone but herself.

"I do!" Alanna wailed. "I love him, but if I move into that apartment, we'll be over in a day. It's *his*, you know? He chose the perfect couch. Every picture is exactly right for the space. It's minimalist. Clean lines, all that crap. There's no room for me and my mismatched stuff." She looked around her room at the bric-a-brac, the colorful wall hangings and the bright scarves draped across the window. "If I move in, I'll wither away like a plant that's been shoved in the back of a dark closet."

She buried her face in her hands. "I love him to bits, but he's put it all out there asking me. Ultracompetent, careful Miles, showing his vulnerable underbelly like this? How can I say no? This stupid apartment thing is going to kill the relationship." Alanna sniffled.

Georgette handed her the box of tissues from the nightstand. Her friend nodded her thanks. "Sorry, I just…" She grimaced at James. "I'm not normally such a crybaby. Great host, right? Seriously, you're welcome to all my cornflakes. I think there's a box of waffles in the back of the freezer too. Living large, that's us." Her smile was wan.

Strangely, Georgette said nothing to help guide her friend.

So James did. The solution was blindingly obvious. At least he could fix someone else's romantic problems, even if he couldn't do a damned thing about his own. "Why don't you find a new place?"

Alanna blinked at him. "What?"

"Go apartment hunting. Sign a lease on an empty apartment the two of you can decorate together. If you can't agree on that, you probably won't make it long-term. If you can, well, then you'll know."

And now he had an image of Georgette laughing

with him at his sister's Lands-End-on-steroids taste in bedroom decor. What would she do, how would she add her style to his place if she had a chance? In the city, she'd dressed sleek and elegant, with blazers and collared shirts, but in Pine Mountain, she'd worn— well, she'd worn his sweater, with nothing underneath.

Longing hit him like a sledgehammer blow. They hadn't had a chance to be together in any normal way, not this time around, and hardly as teenagers, with all the sneaking around. Alanna's talk of moving in with Miles was so normal, it hurt.

He was distracted from his thoughts by a bear hug. Alanna threw herself on him, hugging him with surprising ferocity. "That's it! That's so simple! Brilliant!" She pulled back abruptly. "Uh, sorry." She surveyed his bare chest. "You might want to put something on. Not that I don't like the view, mind you." She winked at Georgette, did an impromptu twirl across the room, then grabbed her phone. "Gotta go make a call." And she was gone, out the bedroom door.

"Is she always that energetic?"

"Alanna? Yeah, pretty much." Georgette pulled his shirt off over her head and presented it to him. "You might want this." She was naked from the waist up. He took the shirt but stroked her shoulder, slid his hand down the concave curve of her back first. She leaned into him with a sigh.

She felt warm and right under his touch, but they were in someone else's apartment. Someone else's bedroom. Borrowed space, borrowed time. And it abruptly felt wrong to be here. To be touching Georgette like this.

Her friend Alanna was agonizing about moving into her boyfriend's apartment because it was designed for him as a solo project, and she couldn't see traces of herself there. Well, Georgette's life was like that too. No room for him. He didn't belong here.

They'd been snowbound in his cabin, and it had been achingly perfect. Now they were here, and she was slipping back into her life. As she should.

Maybe it was already over, this thing they'd had. And maybe that was for the best.

Georgette rummaged in the suitcase they'd rescued from the inn and quickly got dressed. She picked up her phone. "I'm going to call Trudy."

James got up. "I'll see you around."

She thumbed the phone off. "What?"

"I should get going. I'm in the way." He pocketed his phone and his wallet.

"You're really not. This place is a two bedroom, and Jared will be in New Jersey for the rest of the week. I'm sure it would be okay to crash in his room."

He clenched the wallet convulsively in his hand.

"And then what?"

"Is that what this is about?"

"You're back in New York. You can walk." He acknowledged the stick. "Mostly. I've told you everything I know about the accident." *Everything important, anyway.* "You don't need me anymore."

He shouldered his daypack and leaned down to kiss her. Soft, lingering. Imprinting the memory.

She reached up and grabbed on to his shirt collar, pulling him down to her level, next to her on the bed. "Maybe I'm not ready to say good-bye yet." And she turned the kiss into something much deeper, much sexier.

"Hey, guess what? Miles says he'd love to—" Alanna bounced into the room, stopped in the doorway. "Ah, guys? That *is* my bed."

James stood hastily. "Sorry. I'm gone."

Georgette stood too, shakier, grabbing the footboard. "Wait. Let's…"

He waited. *Move in together? Get married? Commit to each other?*

"Explore the city. You don't have to go back today, do you? And they still have all the holiday decorations up for another couple of days. It'll be fun." She gave him a steady look. "And I think we deserve some fun, don't you?" She turned to Alanna. "Can James—" She flushed. "I mean, can *we* stay in Jared's room tonight?"

Alanna grinned. "Sure. Tomorrow night too. What he doesn't know won't hurt him. Just don't be too loud. We do have neighbors."

He should say no. He should go home. He should go mountaineering, lift weights, speed downhill on narrow skis, get her out of his system. But he didn't want that. The restlessness he expected wasn't there. In its place was a tiny shred of...hope.

Maybe this *could* work. Even if she didn't remember everything. Maybe that was okay after all.

James ended up staying two nights. First stop: a New Year's Day brunch at her friend Samantha's boyfriend's apartment. Georgette was tempted to tell James the whole kinky story of how Sam and Dylan had met, but settled for "Jeanine fixed them up," which was technically true, though it left out all the juicy bits. When Sam's boyfriend, Dylan, referred to his lover as Saffron, then seemed embarrassed at the slip, James looked baffled. Across the table, Jeanine winked at Georgette.

James was in full charm mode, cracking jokes that had the whole table laughing and listening intently in the way only he could, and periodically glancing at her, his eyes sparkling, to make sure she was engaged. A perfect date. And for a moment, she pictured a life where this was their norm: getting together with friends on a Sunday for mimosas and banana pancakes after a leisurely, satisfying morning in bed together. In their penthouse apartment in Long Island City, naturally, with a view of Midtown.

Of course, he lived in Pine Mountain, and she was about to move back to New Mexico. It wasn't meant to be. And probably shouldn't be, with so much history between them. But it was a sweet fantasy.

After they said their good-byes and walked out onto West End Avenue in the early winter sunset, James got a text and pumped his fist. "Yes! Ryan says he can do it." He kissed Georgette. "You're going to love this."

"Love what?"

"You'll see." He stepped out into the street, waved down a cab—the man had the magic touch—and gave him an address by the Hudson River Piers.

When they got there, it turned out to be a helipad. James's friend Ryan was a helicopter pilot.

By the time they got up over the city, the sky was deep blue and the city was lit up, the skyscrapers striking silhouettes studded with lights. The top of the Empire State Building was red and green to celebrate the holiday, with the tip streaked with red-and-white stripes like a candy cane. Georgette hugged James. "This is amazing!"

He grinned at her. "Isn't it?" His words got caught

by the hum of the helicopter, but it didn't matter.

The next day, they did the sights, but not the way she and her mother had. No Rockefeller Center or department store windows. Georgette took James to the New York Botanical Garden in the Bronx, where they explored the Holiday Train Show, examining the cleverly designed miniatures of New York City landmarks, then linked arms and strolled—slowly, as Georgette's ankle was still on the mend—through the winter-quiet gardens. For lunch, they went to Arthur Avenue for the freshest mozzarella in the city and the most authentic Italian pizza. Then on to the Metropolitan Museum and the indoor Christmas tree, with its angels and candles and Neapolitan baroque crèche. Gazing at the tree, James whispered in Georgette's ear, "Classy. Can we go now?" So maybe that part wasn't quite as much of a success.

They slept in Jared's bed for the second night in a row and made love quietly, with respect to the neighbors and to Alanna, slumbering in the next room. And it was gentle and tender and achingly sweet, though Georgette bit James's shoulder when she climaxed. Later, he whispered, "Maybe I'll get a tattoo there."

She didn't want to sleep. She wanted to hold on to this moment forever. But even as she drifted off, she knew: it felt this way, like lightning in a bottle, because it was short-term. Intense, like James himself. Destined to burn out like all good things did.

As she drifted off to sleep, the thoughts kept swirling through her brain: *Why? Why say good-bye tomorrow?* And: *Do we have to?*

When James fully woke up, Georgette was gone. She'd gotten up a while ago, saying something about restlessness. He told her that was his line and gathered her in for a soul kiss, but—after a thoroughly satisfying interlude—she pulled away and said she was going to head to the studio, that she missed checking in with her paintings. How could he argue with that? He meant to get up with her, make her a fluffy omelet or maybe even eggs Benedict if Alanna's fridge had the ingredients, but the bed felt cozy and the comforter was warm, and he drifted for another few minutes and then another...

It wasn't altogether surprising that she was gone by the time he wandered out into the main room. She'd left a bagel for him on a plate, neatly sliced, and a mug of strong coffee next to it. And a note.

Correction: a list.

He smiled. One of Georgette's lists.

This one was about him. Or, rather, for him, since it was unlikely she'd accidentally left it on the counter beside the breakfast she'd set out for him.

REASONS IT'S A GOOD IDEA TO BE WITH
JAMES THROUGH THE SPRING

*1) Because he's hot as hell*

*2) Because we have fun together*

*3) Because I'm in* (here something had been crossed
out) *serious like with him.*

*4) Because he makes me laugh*

*5) And think.*

*6) Because I'm not an idiot and I want to enjoy this
remaining time together, not apart*

*7) Because why not?*

REASONS IT'S A BAD IDEA

She'd put a big fat zero, complete with a diagonal
line through it.

This was a keepsake list. The best list she'd ever
written, though he'd kill for a look at the word she'd
crossed out.

The front door opened. James looked up with a
smile.

It wasn't Georgette coming back from the studio.
It was a guy with an awfully familiar face. He wore an
orange wool coat, his dark blond hair was upswept in a
stylish wave, and—

"Jared, right?"

Jared dropped a suitcase and a garment bag by the
door and came over to join James in the kitchen. "And
you're James of the fire escape escapades. Good to see

you, man. Guess this means you and Georgie patched things up."

"Seems like it." James couldn't help himself. He glanced down at the list.

"Oh?" Jared came over to blatantly read over his shoulder. "Better list than the one she wrote about which apartment she should take, the one with the roaches or the basement pad that shook every time the subway went by."

James folded the list and pocketed it. "This one works for me."

"So only the spring, huh? Why's that?"

James took a bite of bagel. "I guess because she's off to her cushy job at that New Mexico spa, and God forbid her priorities change on my account." Ouch. That sounded bitter.

Jared swiped the other half of the bagel. "Give her time. She's trying awfully hard to avoid the L word right now. Typical Georgette, right? Stubborn, leads with the head, not the heart."

"Yeah, well." James got up and tossed the napkin in the trash. This conversation was making him feel restless. And he had a studio to visit. "Thanks for the pep talk."

"Get a drink when you have time?"

"You know it."

# Chapter Twenty

Georgette stripped off her gloves and scarf, setting them on the small table by the door. She kept her coat on for now. The air in the studio felt chilly, with Finn's kitchen downstairs dormant for the holidays.

It felt good to be back in the familiar space. Not that she planned to paint—at least, probably not. She didn't have any new dream fragments pressing in on her, and the real James was more about kisses and shared moments than images she had to capture. But after she'd written that list, she'd had to get out of the apartment before James saw it.

Even thinking of it now—she pressed her chilled hands to her overheated face. It wasn't a mash note, but it might as well be. It felt so…

Maybe she should run back over to Alanna's and snatch it off the counter before James woke up.

Then again, maybe he'd already seen it. Maybe she'd walk in on him reading it. It felt so…

Vulnerable.

And Georgette Soren didn't do vulnerable.

She walked with care—her ankle was almost healed, barely tender—over to her stack of paintings. The set she'd done of James when he was her mystery man.

She'd looked at them so many times, she could close her eyes and see every detail. And yet she needed to see them again. Oils on primed canvas, striated brushstrokes in olives, ochres, skin tones. They shouldn't mean as much as they did.

She pulled the first painting out, the one of James as a teenager on the edge of the ravine, and set it aside.

The second, the one of James as a teenager, laughing into the wind, his hair rough, his smile wide, his eyes alight. She set it aside too.

The next one, James, distraught, crouching in an empty room. Georgette inhaled. The space. She recognized the wide window ledge, the suggestion of a closet by the side wall. The dimensions fit. She'd painted her Pine Mountain home without even realizing it. Her old bedroom. Was it a metaphor? It had to be. She'd left him behind in her old life. He'd been boxed away in her subconscious. Powerful imagery. She stepped back. This one was hard to look at now.

She took out the fourth canvas and set it against the wall. This one was of James, grown into full manhood. Sitting on a subway bench, his head in his hands, the picture of despair. This one made no sense. She'd painted him like this, and then she'd witnessed it. Coincidence? Had to be. The subway too was a metaphor, no doubt a stand-in for his arrival in New

York, bringing painful memories along with him.

Had to be that. Nothing else made sense. Nothing else was logical.

On to the fifth canvas.

She recoiled. It wasn't that she'd forgotten the painting. How could she? But it meant something so different now.

A tapping sound came from behind her. From the window.

She went on alert.

The tapping sound came again, insistent.

No way. He hadn't.

She turned to look.

Oh, but he had.

James rapped again. His grin flashed white behind the glass.

Georgette grabbed the walking stick even though she probably didn't need it, and went over to open the window and let him in.

It slid up easily this time, and he stepped inside.

"You could have used the stairs." She heard the wobble in her voice, the freeze.

James kissed her exuberantly, his mouth warm but his lips chilled. "What's the fun in that?"

Something was off. Georgette wasn't responding to his kiss, wasn't smiling at his playful teasing. He pulled back and examined her face, running his finger along the center of her forehead to smooth the worry line. "Having second thoughts? Going to send me on my way after all?"

Georgette stepped back, arms folded, self-protective. What was going on? "No, I want to be with you. It's just that…" She picked up a canvas by the top stretcher bar and brought it into the center of the room.

When she propped it up on an easel and stepped away, James felt a sickening jolt. "That's me?"

"I've had this dream twice. Once before I met you, once…"

"At my cabin."

"The second night."

The night she'd cried his name in her sleep, her voice strangled with fear. The night he'd stood by her bed, stroking her hair, but it didn't still her thrashing, her anguished expression. The night he'd slid under the comforter, nestling her against him, giving her comfort the only way he could.

The night she'd woken in his arms, comfort turned to passion, and they made love for the first time.

That night.

"This was your dream?" He gestured to the painting. A figure with a familiar leather jacket was sprawled on the cement sidewalk, his body contorted like he'd broken his spine. Skyscrapers surrounded him, looming like distorted giants. Red and blue lights strafed the edges of the frame, silhouettes of witnesses surrounded the body at the center.

*His* body.

"Not exactly. This was from the first dream. In the one I had that night in Pine Mountain, you were falling. You had a camera. I was falling with you, and then it turned into the gorge here." She blinked. Tears? "I can't—your job. I think it's about your job."

"Oh, Georgie." He reached her in a single stride, held her close against his chest. He could feel her trembling, her stuttering breaths. She was genuinely shaken.

He pulled back, gently brushed a stray lock of hair off her face. "I've been at *Adrenaline Rush* full time for the past four years, and I'm still in one piece. There are safeguards. Everything's vetted. No accidents."

Well, if you didn't count the time he'd capsized on a run down the Zambezi River, ruining half his gear and nearly grinding himself on the rocks before he escaped the powerful currents. Or the time his chute didn't open fast enough on a jump over the Rockies. But those details weren't going to help Georgette feel better.

She gave him a wet smile. "Still. It's dangerous. Obviously. And my subconscious knows it."

"I'm glad your subconscious cares so much." He kissed her nose. She tilted her head, and it turned into a real kiss. He pulled her against him, letting her feel his arousal, and glanced around the room. Sex in an art studio? Why not? He could hoist her onto that long table...

She murmured against his mouth. "You don't need to do that anymore, right? Those daredevil stunts. Now that you and I have reconciled, you can let go of that."

He pulled back to look at her face. "Are you saying you cured me?"

"Not that." She flushed. "But you have to admit, it's better. Wasn't the thrill seeking about the trauma of —of what happened at the reservoir? And that's resolved now. Isn't it? I mean..." She gestured between them. "Us, our time together, it's helped. Both of us."

And it was true. He hadn't felt that telltale restless itchiness under his skin for days. Being with Georgette had brought a measure of peace.

Still, her words didn't sit right. "You sound like this—us—it's *therapy*." The window behind him was still cracked open, and a cold breeze stole inside, brushing his hair and creeping into his chest. "Is that why you're with me? Is that why we got together?"

Georgette limped to the window and yanked it shut, then grabbed a rag from a nearby easel and wiped

her hands. "Of course. That's why I went up to Pine
Mountain in the first place. It's been extremely
therapeutic."

"Is that it? Is that the only reason?"

She flushed and glanced away. "I'm attracted to
you. You know that. I like being with you."

"But we've got an expiration date. Come
graduation day, June whatever, you're on a plane to
that fancy desert spa."

"It's a good job. A solid foundation. Maybe not
that exciting, but that's okay by me." She tossed the rag
on the table. "What do you expect me to do? Give up
my career and move in with you, pining away in Pine
Mountain while you go off and risk your neck every
few months? Throw away my five-year plan on a
whim? That's not logical."

And there it was. Logic.

He strode across the space, not sure until he got
there whether he was about to strangle her or kiss
some sense into her. He settled for grabbing her by the
shoulders. Their connection sparked, unwilling and
unlooked for.

Georgette clearly felt it too. She inhaled sharply
and looked away.

"Look at me. Look me in the eyes and tell me we
have no future. Tell me you feel nothing for me, that
this is just an extended therapy session."

She winced, and he belatedly realized he was digging his fingers into her shoulders. Her muscles under his touch felt tight. Breakable. He willed himself to relax his grip.

"I don't think that. That's why I wrote that list. I thought—June is a long time from now. I thought we could have fun."

"Fun. So we can have *fun* for the spring and just the spring, but only if I agree to stop taking dangerous jobs? You don't change anything, and it's a short-term affair, but I have to give everything up?" He let go of her and stepped away, bitterness welling up in his chest.

"It's not for me. It's for your own safety."

"Uh-huh. Because there's no *us.*" He should have known. This interlude had been too good to be true. His mother was right, dammit. "So the paintings, the dreams, they were all just your subconscious knocking at the door, telling you to remember what went down ten years ago, it's time to get past it?"

"Of course that's what it was. That's how the brain works. What else could it be?"

"Oh, I don't know. Some people might think it was significant that you dreamed about me like this"— he pointed to the painting of himself on the subway platform—"and then it happened. Right down to my bomber jacket."

"Lucky guess." Her voice wobbled. "It's very you, that jacket."

"Of course. Because we're not connected by anything more than attraction and the past. If I feel more, I'm deluding myself. Have you wondered why I happened to stop by the reservoir last week? Not exactly a popular hike in midwinter. It was no coincidence. I was sitting at dinner with my family and I got this strange feeling, this compulsion. I knew something was wrong, and I had to go. Good thing I did, huh?"

Georgette looked stunned. "I didn't know that. That's..." She shook her head, clearly unable to process it. Unable, or unwilling?

He continued, feeling savage. "But it still doesn't mean anything, right? Because we're not soul mates. We weren't destined to find each other again. We don't belong together in some mysterious way because that wouldn't be *logical*. Everything that's gone down this past month, it's all happenstance and therapy."

"I..." Georgette stopped. Leaning heavily on her walking stick, she went to a stool and sat. He cursed himself for a callous fool. She was still healing. "I don't know. It meant more. It means more. But..."

"How much more?"

"I don't know. I can't quantify it. It's..." She shook her head. "Like I said. You mean something to me,

# Chapter Twenty-Two

James stood in the clearing by the precipice, watching her. Her lips still felt the imprint of their kiss. Her heart still vibrated with the giddiness of their reunion. She'd walked out her door and told her parents to suck it when they asked where she was going. Everything was going to be different now. She was sixteen, and she was her own woman, not their puppet. She wanted to be with James? Well, she'd be with James.

But he'd pulled back from their kiss and said, *"I have to tell you something."* His expression so earnest as he explained that he hadn't expected her to come back. He'd thought he lost her. He was hurting. So he had... Here he took a pause, a stalling breath, but then he finally came out with it. *"I slept with Kim. Last month. I don't love her. I love you. If I'd known you'd come back to me..."*

His face, so tender, like he was offering his heart on a platter. She wanted to smack him. Pummel him. Run away and hide, curl up under a tree and sob. It wasn't just about Kim, though she'd always clearly had a thing for James. A kiss, that would have been—well, not okay, but manageable. She could get her brain around a kiss. This wasn't that.

Sex.

They'd never done it. They'd teased each other right up to the moment of decision but always pulled back. She hadn't been ready. He'd said he wasn't either. They'd both agreed they would lose their virginity together. They would be each other's firsts. But not yet. Not until they were sure.

But now...now she'd always be the one who hadn't.

She swung around, toward the cliff edge. Dancing right up to it. *"That's okay,"* she said. *"Sleep with her again. Take her to prom this year. Marry her. I didn't bring you here to get back together. I brought you here to show you this."* She struggled with the heavy ring he'd given her for her birthday, the one she'd taken out of her jewelry box this morning and slid onto her finger with a frisson of delight. Now she yanked it off, pulling at her skin along with the silver-coated metal. She meant to hold it up, then symbolically toss it into the reservoir so far below them, like Frodo tossing the Ring into the Crack of Doom—but like Frodo, she couldn't.

The ring was stuck. But how awful to explain, with James standing there. What a humiliating anticlimax, to simply walk away. She yanked on the damned thing harder, dancing backward as she did, not paying attention to where she stepped until—

okay? You do."

"Mmm." It was like picking a scab. He knew he shouldn't, but he couldn't help it. "So if I were to say fine, I'll quit my *Adrenaline Rush* gig and open a shop in Pine Mountain, one of those places that shoot weddings and puppies and school yearbook photos, if I were to do that, would you be happy? Would you say no to the spa job?"

She opened her mouth, probably about to equivocate or tell him why that was a bad idea, or tell him she might consider it but only with some big huge catch that would ruin everything.

He went on in a rush. "Would you marry me and pop out babies, say five in a row? Or, no, seven. I always wanted a big family." He was pushing it. He should shut up and make nice or risk the next few months of precarious happiness, all she had to offer him.

*Screw it.* He'd be watching the days and minutes tick past. Better to toss it all away now rather than live through that.

She said nothing. She didn't have to. Her face said it all. Fear, tightness, rejection.

So he said it for her. "Of course you wouldn't. You're thinking about my well-being, that's all. Not about any future we might have together. God forbid I want to be together after your June cutoff. Because you have a plan. A master list, and I'm not on it. No, I get it." He turned toward the window. "Don't worry, I'll let myself out."

"Don't go. Not like this."

The restlessness was back, but this time it was more of an urge to smash things. He had to get out of here before he punched a hole through every one of her precious paintings.

He slid the window all the way up, then turned back to Georgette. "I think you took the wrong lesson from what happened to you. You learned to be afraid. To dole everything out in measured scoops. Including your heart. You want me to stop taking risks? Of course you do. You don't take enough."

He left before he could say anything more. It already hurt too much. So much for her sweet list from this morning. So much for hope.

He climbed down the fire escape, taking the steps two and three at a time, wishing he had a rope so he could scale down the wall. Contemplating jumping in the East River, but he'd probably die of hypothermia before someone could come rescue him, and that would prove Georgette's point.

Instead he went home. Back to Alanna's to collect his things, avoiding Jared's sympathetic glances, then back on the road. It was over. It was truly over. And he had to get away before he broke down.

The cold air wafted in from the still-open window. Georgette didn't move.

Her stomach turned over, protesting lack of food. Georgette didn't care.

She should go back to the apartment. She should look for a place to live, dig into the pile of work she'd blown off while she was in Pine Mountain playing house with James. She should at least get up off the floor. She didn't.

The floor was soothing. Reliably solid. She'd gotten up from the stool after James left, intending to close the window, but instead, she'd settled on the floor. Just for a moment. Until she regained her equilibrium.

That was half an hour ago.

She ran her hands across the pale gray concrete, cool and smooth under her palms. With her back against the wall, she could be comfortable here for hours. Maybe years. Why not? She could do phone consults to make money, order pizza, and sit on this floor. Stay in this safe warehouse space, surrounded by the shapes and canvases conjured by her friends' creative impulses.

As for her? She'd probably never paint again. It caused too much trouble.

She'd certainly never fall in love. As James said, too

dangerous.

The thought itself hurt, like shards of ice stabbing her in the heart, then melting away, leaving no trace behind.

James. His messy hair, his intent gaze, his beloved mouth. Out the window, down the fire escape. Gone.

She should get up. She should move on too.

She didn't.

A key turned in the lock.

Alanna came in, walking in her usual rush. She paused with her coat half-off, did a double take. "Georgette? What are you doing on the floor? Are you okay?" She shrugged the coat off and let it drop onto the floor, hurrying over to Georgette. "I thought you were off exploring the city with lover boy, being photogenic on the Brooklyn Bridge and whatnot." She knelt in front of her.

"He's gone."

Alanna followed Georgette's glance to the window. "The fire escape again? That boy." She got up and went to close it, then came back, eyeing Georgette. "You okay? Dumb question, scratch that. What happened?"

"I blew it. I thought we could have a spring fling, but then I asked for too much from him, and it boomeranged back at me."

"Uh... You'll have to be more specific. What boomeranged? Did someone use the L word?"

The door opened again, and Hayley came in, brushing a light coating of white off her hair. "It's snowing again, did you know that?" Like Alanna before her, she paused, her scarf unwrapped but her coat still on. "What's going on? You break something?"

Alanna said, "Yeah, her heart."

Georgette added, "Which I don't have, apparently."

Hayley hung her coat up. "Ouch. This that hot guy from Roman's party?"

Behind her, Susannah came in, looking around cautiously, as if she expected a stranger to jump out at her. Her gaze darted to Georgette and Alanna. "Hi."

"Hi." Alanna sketched a wave.

Georgette didn't have the energy, so she summoned a wan smile.

Not bothering to hang up her coat or drop her bag, Suzu came straight over to where Georgette sat against the wall. She crouched in front of her and took both hands. "Whatever this is, it's going to get better. You need to know that." She sounded so earnest, Georgette couldn't help but smile, this time for real.

She patted Suzu's hands back. "I know. I mean, I should know. That's logical. The heart mends, we're resilient that way. I've just never felt this way before. It's...unexpected."

Hayley went to a shrouded sculpture in the middle

of the room and threw off the tarp, surveying it critically. It was an abstract figure, all angles and sharp lines. "Let's order pizza and diss men. That'll cheer you up."

"Hey, not all men are bad," Alanna said.

Hayley walked around to the other side of her sculpture, surveying it. "Fine, we'll make an exception for Perfect Miles. Does this look too much like a human figure to you?"

Alanna blinked. "Uh, no?"

Georgette stirred. "James isn't a bad guy. He's..." The paintings still leaned against the far wall, multifaceted James in painted form. All she had left. "He's intense, moody, sometimes strange, sometimes wild. But he's got a huge heart, and he'd risk his own life to save you. And he knows how to live fully. And that's no small thing." James carrying her upstairs. James teasing her. James whirling around after she'd smacked in the back of the neck with a snowball. James making love to her, his face taut, tender, filled with light.

Georgette came back to the present to find the other three women staring at her.

"Well, damn, woman. If you're that in love with him, go after him," Hayley said.

Alanna nodded. "Do it. I know it's hard, but it's worth it. Trust me."

Georgette put her head between her knees. It felt peaceful here, with her friends around her and the smell of turpentine permeating the air. "It's not that simple. As he pointed out, he's not about to leave his job, and I can't stomach the danger. And what am I going to do, destroy my plans? Is a man more important than my career?"

Hayley nodded. "Woman's got a point." She picked up her phone. "Two pizzas, or three?"

The conversation switched to toppings and size and slices, and extra cheese, or garlic? And Georgette got up and went to the paintings. *These paintings.* The ones that caused so much trouble. The ones that blew her life wide open, but not wide enough. She still didn't remember everything.

She turned around. "You want to hear something weird?"

Hayley was on the phone. Suzu was perched on the window ledge. Alanna still sat on the floor where Georgette had been.

Alanna cocked her head. "Sure. What?"

"James thinks the dreams aren't just memories and symbols. He thinks they mean we're meant to be together." It felt stupidly vulnerable even saying it. "How can I be with a man who makes us out to have some huge mystical connection?" She left out the part where he'd sensed her terror and need at the reservoir fence, because that felt like a dream too. Like the kind of story your brain tells you after the fact to make things feel more dramatic. Because it couldn't have happened that way.

*Could it?*

Alanna came over and wrapped her arms around Georgette. "Sweetie, that's what love is. A connection between two people is an amazing thing. Practically unexplainable."

Georgette shook her head. "It isn't. It can't be." Love was a biological imperative, a cultural need to have companionship.

It wasn't supposed to hurt this much.

She'd get used to it. He'd fade into the past. Because she couldn't give up everything to be with a man who wasn't willing to give up anything.

And she couldn't be in love. Stripped bare. Vulnerable.

Georgette was eminently practical. Love wasn't.

James wasn't.

She couldn't be with him. She shouldn't be with him.

# Chapter Twenty-One

She didn't get over it. January, March, April...
nope. Not long enough, apparently. She should be
better by now. Thoughts of James shouldn't still make
her feel turned inside out.

He'd gotten into her head. She hadn't had any new
dreams, though. At least, not the vivid memory kind.
Plenty of the other kind, dreams of James coming back
to New York, showing up in her studio, saying he took
everything back, he'd be with her on her terms. James
in the snow, standing with his arms outstretched as she
ran into his embrace.

Dreams. Fantasies. Comfort.

She'd hold on to the thoughts as she fell asleep,
but she never mentioned them to anyone, and she
certainly never painted any of those images. In fact,
she hadn't been back to the studio in three months.
Alanna had even stopped pestering her to show up,
that was how long it had been.

James was still in her head. Case in point:

She threaded her way through the upscale Water
of Life Spa, following Dawn, her tour guide and
prospective employer, past rooms where women and
men—but mostly women—lay on beds with
cucumbers on their eyes and their hair wrapped in

towels; past the swimming pool where women and men—but mostly women—were doing laps; past the sauna, where they baked, and the steam room, where they boiled; past the meditation room, where they banged on gongs and chanted in unison. It was beautiful here, with skylights and bleached wood everywhere and a profusion of hanging ferns. It would be a lovely place to work. A peaceful, controlled environment, where her clients would be eager to change and grow and reveal themselves in stages.

And yet as she sat down across from Dawn in her plush office, Georgette found herself saying, "I'm not sure this is the right place for me." And, "I'm thinking about taking a different direction in my work."

Dawn cocked her head, very much as Alanna would, though her sleek blonde hair was back in a bun instead of falling across her face like Alanna's always did. "And what direction is that?" Her voice was cultured and soothing, the consummate trained therapist.

"Something with kids, I think. Teenagers."

Dawn pursed her mouth. "They're so messy. Emotionally."

"Exactly." Georgette smiled at her. "I can make a real difference there. Your clients, pardon me for saying so—they've mostly got it together. I want to go where I'm needed."

And it felt right. Throwing out her five-year plan, following her gut. James would be proud.

Not that she was thinking about him.

Not for at least five minutes, anyway.

The hardest part came after, when she arrived back at her parents' sprawling Mediterranean-influenced house. Her mother met her at the door, ready with a cocktail and a beaming smile.

Georgette drank the martini for courage, then sat her mother down and told her she'd decided not to take the job after all, that it wasn't who she was. "I love you, but I feel like you've been trying to protect me from myself for a long time. Most of my life. I'm not you. I'm not going to fall apart. And even if I do, that's my problem. Let me."

Her mother started crying. When Georgette tried hugging her, she cried harder. When Georgette tried apologizing, Sally wiped her eyes and said, "Do you hate me, then?"

Georgette sat back in her chair. "No! Of course not." Even though maybe she did, a little. "It's going to take some time for me to get past what you did, that's all."

"You mean not telling you about that boy?"

"I think it's called lying."

"We never lied. Well, mostly not. You didn't remember. We simply left out that part of your life in the retelling."

"But last December, when he reappeared. You lied then."

Her mother didn't answer at first, and Georgette thought maybe she wasn't going to. That she'd pushed too far. That she'd broken something.

Finally, her mother said, "I'm sorry." Her voice was such a soft thread, Georgette could barely hear her. "I didn't want to lose you. I thought you'd be furious."

"So you lied."

Her mother bent her head. "So I lied."

Georgette spent another two days at her parents' house. Swimming, arguing, and talking honestly and openly for the first time, maybe ever. Healing.

Three months. Three long months, watching the snow deepen and then melt, watching the trees begin to bud, the barest promise of spring.

In February, James flew to Peru to film a bunch of rowdy sand boarders tackling the giant dunes in Huacachina. He was in a sand buggy, someone else was driving, and he thought, *See, Georgette, it's exhilarating and joyous and perfectly safe*. But when he got out of the car, his legs were shaky and his endorphins flatlined. When the gig wasn't fun anymore, it was simply work.

He tipped his canister to his mouth, drank lukewarm water as the sun set over the huge expanse of desert, and tried not to think about how it would feel to have her with him right now, nestled against him, commenting on the view.

In March, James flew to Utah to shoot a crew descending into the slot canyons in Zion, but the mission was scrubbed when a flash flood came through. He sat at a Mexican restaurant in Springdale with the group, drinking margaritas and eating guacamole and chips, and thought, *See, Georgette, we take precautions.* And tried to ignore the tickle of relief that he hadn't needed to go in there and risk his neck.

In April, he went down to New York City a day ahead of schedule before the Jersey City shoot. He took a PATH train into Manhattan, walked around the city, and tried not to think about New Year's and Georgette. When he found himself staring at a subway map, looking for the approximate spot in Greenpoint where Finn's Fermentation Factory was, he turned away.

He could find her, sure. Climb up the fire escape one more time. But she'd made her decision. She was out of his life.

At some point in the distant future, he'd look back at their winter interlude as closure and absolution and all good things, and if he ran into her on the street, he'd give her a wistful kiss on the cheek and walk away feeling a mildly pleasant melancholy. But not yet.

He stayed away.

He did, however, go to the *Adrenaline Rush* office and have a long-overdue conversation with Maggie and the editor-in-chief.

And then it was time to prepare for the wingsuit shoot.

Up here on the skyscraper roof, it felt like winter, with the breeze stinging his cheeks. Next to him, Blake, the lead glider, leaned over the edge, looking down. "Whoa, long way, isn't it?" He took a few shots with his camera phone, then turned it around for a selfie with James. "Sweet, huh?"

"Yeah. So you'll need to jump from there." James pointed to the ledge beside them. "That way, I can get a good shot before I take off myself."

"Sure, mate, we can do that."

Blake went off to confer with his partners.

Behind him, Maggie wrapped her arms around herself, looking chilled in her thin suede jacket. James shed his bomber jacket and set it across her shoulders.

She nodded her thanks. "You're committed to this being your last shoot for us? I hope you'll reconsider."

"Sorry, yeah. It's time to move on."

"You'll miss the adrenaline rush. You love danger. You'll be back." She gave him a flirtatious look from under her long eyelashes. He felt nothing. She was an attractive woman. Intelligent. Clearly available. And he felt nothing.

He turned away, back to Blake and the plans for tomorrow's jump. The thrill was gone. Georgette had been right.

*Georgette.* Her name conjured up an image of her —windswept hair blowing in her eyes, her cheeks pink with cold and embarrassment, her mouth red from his kisses.

His Georgette.

Dammit. Not his.

Alanna scooted around the desk in the corner of her former bedroom. "Sorry. I'll be out of your way in a few."

"No problem. It's your place." Georgette picked up the laptop and moved to the bed.

"Was. It's yours now." Alanna had unofficially moved in with Miles in February, but kept her stuff here. They'd signed a lease on a two bedroom in Williamsburg in March, and were finally moving in, after many intensive debates about furniture and decor.

"As long as Jared doesn't kick me out."

"You kidding? He was so relieved when you said you weren't moving to New Mexico, he made himself three sandwiches. He's too lazy to scout around for a new roommate. You solved the problem." Alanna dumped a pile of scarves into a box and shoved them down, then went to the closet.

"Now I need a job."

"You'll find something. Sooner rather than later, I can feel it." Alanna emerged from the closet with two pairs of boots, which she tossed across the room. They sailed straight into the box on top of the scarves. "Slam dunk! Am I good or what?"

A message popped up in Georgette's email, from her high school friend Theresa. They'd started chatting after her Pine Mountain sojourn.

"Looks like you may be right about finding that job." Georgette skimmed the email.

"See? I have magic powers. What's the gig?"

"Apparently I can apply for a position as the school psychologist in Pine Mountain. How weird would that be?"

Alanna paused, a high-heeled boot in her hand. "Would you?"

*Pine Mountain. The clean air, the sweet main street. James.*

"I don't know if it's a good idea. Not while I'm still hung up on James."

Alanna's shoe sailed across the room and into the box. The heel snagged on the edge. "True love is hard to move past."

"Says the inveterate romantic." *James*. What was he doing right now? Giving in to the compulsion, she pulled down her browser's history menu and found the *Adrenaline Rush* magazine website. She hadn't looked at it since last week. Maybe there was something new.

Not on the main page. She'd seen all these. They'd published an article in February with James's photos in it, a motocross championship race in France in November. A box at the bottom of the piece explained how James had ridden in a special race car alongside the motorcyclists so he could shoot video of them on the go. The image of him hanging out the car window was disturbing enough that Georgette kept away from the *Adrenaline Rush* website for an entire month. But she came back. James wasn't on Twitter, and she wasn't about to friend him on Facebook. This was her only glimpse into his life.

Alanna grabbed a bundle of skirts and carried them to the box, which was rapidly becoming overstuffed. Georgette skimmed the *Adrenaline Rush* website. The right sidebar was new. It had blogs, it looked like. And one of the blogs…

She clicked.

A guy named Blake was writing in a breezy tone about how they were going BASE jumping off the top of the building at 99 Hudson in Jersey City tomorrow at four p.m.—seriously sweet, right? He included some images from what he called the setup day.

James was in one, squinting into the camera alongside a dark-skinned Aboriginal guy in his early twenties, presumably Blake. Georgette drank in the image. This was what James looked like right now. Scruffy, like he was considering growing in a beard but hadn't decided yet. His hair was as messy as ever, his bomber jacket unzipped, his expression unusually guarded. Taken today? She checked the byline. Yesterday.

She clicked through the rest of the slideshow eagerly, scanning for James, and found him in one more, a wider angle. James was talking with that woman from the magazine office. She wore his jacket. Georgette suppressed a bitter flash of jealousy. No point. He wasn't hers.

Then she saw it, and her body went cold.

The background. Skyscrapers, steel and blue and tan. The downtown Manhattan skyline past the Hudson River.

It was the same as her dream. The one where James was... James was...

*Dead. Splattered on the concrete, his spine twisted.*

She got up, stumbled across the room. "Where are my..." She shoved a pair of boots on without looking.

Alanna stood by the door, holding a box of books, frowning at Georgette. "What's going on? What other, both laid bare.

As their wrangler called out the countdown, "Five!" James checked his camera harness.

"Four!" James checked on the drone. It swooped and soared a few feet off the ledge, ready to dive with them.

"Three!" James checked his parachute release.

As the wrangler called, "Two!" a woman simultaneously shouted, "James!" Her words were caught by the wind, practically inaudible.

He didn't look. Who would interrupt the count? Everyone here knew the intense focus the gliders needed right before the jump.

"One!"

The other voice was silent.

Oh, hell.

He looked.

Georgette teetered on the ledge a foot away.

*Georgette.*

But she wasn't gazing at him in reproach, she was looking down—overbalancing, about to—

*Oh God.* She was going to fall. With no parachute, no wingsuit. She was going to plummet down to the street. Break all her bones. Break her neck.

*Georgette.*

Oblivious, the wrangler called out, "Now!"

A split-second decision that was no decision at all.

The gliders leaped off the roof.

James leaped—but not off the roof. Toward Georgette.

She fell. She lost her footing and went plummeting down the chasm, her hands grabbing air, the same air that stole her breath—down down down —fast and slow both, an eternity measured in fractions of a second, the rest of her life in a dropperful of moments.

Her heart was pounding so hard, her ears buzzed with the roar of blood churning through her veins, a giddy rush, a terror so vivid, it almost felt like ecstasy.

She pitched forward and fell, the hot air stealing her breath, the rocky outcroppings too far, too slick to grab.

She was about to die.

She fell. She pitched forward and hurtled down into the gorge.

She didn't fall. She felt arms around her, felt an inexorable force yank her back, and she fell backward in a heap with him. Smacking against him, sprawling together on the ground—

Not the ground.

The roof. James had pulled her off the ledge in time.

She wasn't sixteen, this wasn't summer, they weren't at the gorge.

She was alive. Unbroken.

And so was he. In rescuing her, he'd freed himself

from his fate. He hadn't jumped.

She touched James's face, felt his stubble. "You're alive."

He rolled away and sat up. "What the hell were you doing here?"

"Saving your life."

His heart was still pounding, his back was bruised, and his favorite jacket had a tear in it, but he'd caught her in time. He wanted to hug her, shake her, ask her what the hell she'd been thinking.

But for some reason, all he could think to say was, "You made me screw up my job." Because the crew might be focused on the jumpers now, but Maggie would come over soon enough and tear him a new one. "And you tell me it's because—" He belatedly processed her words. *"Saving your life."* His mind went blank. "What?"

She rubbed her face, looking beautifully disheveled and utterly unlike her usual controlled self. "The dream. That painting, remember it? Of you on the ground. It was about this. Here." She gestured around them. "I saw your photo on that guy's blog. The background, it was from my painting. I had to stop you from—from—" She gestured toward the edge. "I sound crazy, don't I?"

He laughed. "Completely."

Once he started laughing, he couldn't stop. He hadn't seen Georgette in three months, they'd said good-bye in such a final way—and yet she'd gotten on a train and come all the way here. Because of a photo. And a dream.

It was so amazingly insane. She'd nearly died up on that ledge. He'd almost had to watch again, helpless as she plummeted—but this time, she'd be crashing onto concrete and there'd be no second chances.

He laughed because it beat crying or screaming or running around tearing his hair out. He laughed because his heart was still pounding from fear and urgency, his body ached from their crash landing on the roof, and he wanted to shake Georgette and kiss her and—

She smacked him on the arm. "Stop it! Don't laugh at me! I can't help it that I love you enough to actually, God forbid, want to prevent your sorry bones from being pulverized on the sidewalk!"

He stopped laughing. "Love?"

She scrambled to her feet. "Forget I said that. Too bad about the gig, but you couldn't very well have collected the money if they had to scrape you off the sidewalk. Have a good life. Forgive me for saving your ass."

She started off across the roof toward the stairwell, but he rose quickly and caught up with her. "You can't say something like that and then walk away."

She swung around. "What does it matter? You get over me quickly enough, don't you? You slept with Kim last time we broke up. Who did you sleep with this time? That woman from your office?"

He stopped dead, his hand on her arm forcing her to stop too. "You remembered, then."

Behind them, a cheer went up. The gliders must have landed safely on the boat.

Georgette's hair blew across her face. She impatiently brushed it away. "Everything."

"Then you have to know Kim meant nothing to me. I had no idea you would change your mind." Good God, a ten-year-old mistake was going to kill his chances at happiness? Please let it not be so.

James looked so stricken, Georgette had to relent. "Of course. I'm not sixteen anymore, and that was a long time ago. I realize it was teenage hormones. Incidentally, I wasn't trying to kill myself. I was trying to take off your damned class ring."

He looked stunned. "You... My ring? All this time, I thought..." He shook his head. "My ring."

She eyed him. "Don't laugh again."

"Wouldn't dream of it." The look in his eye said he was about to kiss her.

She couldn't let that happen. Not yet. "I

understand if there's something between you and that woman. But I need to know."

"What woman?" He seemed genuinely confused.

She gestured toward his sexy colleague, who was currently marching toward them across the expanse of roof, looking mightily pissed off.

He didn't deign to look, and that reassured her even more than his words. "Maggie? There's nothing. Hasn't been. Won't be, especially if you're around—but you're still going to that spa, so this is just a rescue and run."

Georgette swallowed. The wash of reckless determination she'd felt on her way here would come in handy right about now. "I turned it down."

"You…did?" His usually transparent face was opaque, God help her.

"Theresa told me about a job opening at Pine Mountain High. They need a new school psychologist. I'm thinking of applying. I love the town."

And then she held her breath.

But before a stunned James could respond, the magazine woman—Maggie—marched up to them. "What the hell kind of stunt was that? If you hadn't quit, I'd fire you!"

*If he hadn't quit?*

James regarded Maggie with such cool distance, Georgette knew he'd been honest. There was nothing between him and this woman. "You've got enough footage from the drone cam, plus the GoPros on Blake's and Stephan's helmets, not to mention Louis and his telephoto zoom on the boat. You should be fine."

"That's not the point! We hired you for your unique shots. You get right there in with the guys, you catch the best material. You let me down. I could sue you for breach of contract."

"You could. But you won't. I had a choice to make. Go ahead with the jump or save the love of my life from certain death. For some reason, I chose the latter. Go figure." James slanted a look at Georgette, and her heart stuttered. *The love of his life?*

"What are you talking about?" Maggie seemed to register Georgette's presence for the first time. "Where'd she come from?"

"She was up on the ledge. Didn't you notice?"

Maggie blinked hard. "Uh…" Apparently, she'd been so focused on the drone and the jump, she hadn't even seen Georgette's near-disaster. None of them had.

After a brief, fraught conversation, Maggie left to pack up and head out to meet the boat, but she gave James a sidelong wistful look as she walked away. Too bad for her.

James grabbed Georgette's hand. "Let's get out of here before everyone descends."

"Where to?"

They ended up on a boardwalk by the Hudson River. James had changed out of his wingsuit, and was wearing his familiar leather bomber jacket. Georgette leaned against him for protection against the chill wind. He wrapped her in his arms, putting his chin on the top of her head.

It felt right. Snug. Perfect. And it enabled her to ask the question that had been on her mind since Maggie walked away from them. "I'm the love of your life, huh?"

She felt a light whisper of a kiss on the back of her neck, and her entire body lit up. "You knew that, didn't you? I've never pretended otherwise. But what's this about Pine Mountain High? School psychologist? You'll love it."

"Assuming I get the job."

"You'll get the job." She could feel the pulse of his exhale against her back.

"How can you be sure?"

"I know people. And I know you."

She turned in his arms, needing to see his face. The familiar, now-welcome connection flared between them. Could it be this easy? After all that? What was the catch? "You really walked away from *Adrenaline Rush*? What are you going to do? Open that shop on

Main Street and shoot weddings and baptisms?"

"Sure, after we have those five kids." His eyes gleamed.

"Uh, about that."

"Seven, then. If you insist."

She snorted. "I'll have a job."

"Maybe we should only have one or two, then. After all, I'll be traveling for work."

She tensed. "I thought…"

He put his finger on her lips. "You thought right. No more extreme sports. *National Geographic* hired me for a shoot in the Canadian Rockies this summer. I'll be hiking to get the images. Not even rock climbing, I promise."

She exhaled. But… "Is that enough? Will you be satisfied?"

He gave her his light-up-the-world smile, and she knew it was going to be okay. "I'll love it, are you kidding?" He kissed her nose. "Will you come with me sometimes? We can go spelunking, go down the Amazon in big, safe boats. Explore the world."

"On school vacations?"

"Sure. On school vacations." He pulled away for a moment, looking serious. "Is this for real? Us? Are you honestly going to be satisfied living in a cabin in the Adirondacks, working with annoying teenagers? What about the excitement of the city? What about your art?"

A boat horn sang out, echoing across the water. "I love New York. Almost as much as I love Pine Mountain. But we'll come visit, right?"

"And your paintings?"

She pictured James's house. The expanse of meadow around it. "Build me an art studio."

"Done." Then he grinned, sly and mischievous. "So if we're going to have those seven kids, we better get started, don't you think?"

He kissed her. She went up on tiptoe and kissed him back. And it was toe curling and delicious, but it was also tender and sweet and filled with all the love she'd never known she wanted, and her heart felt like it was about to burst, and she didn't think of a single list item, pro or con. Not one. Because she was home. With James. Ready for whatever adventures lay ahead.

# Author Note

Thank you for reading *Warm Me Up*. I hope you enjoyed it. If you want a peek into Georgette's and James's future, I've written an epilogue, which I'm giving away to newsletter subscribers. You can subscribe on my website.

Please consider leaving a review on Amazon and/ or Goodreads. They help other readers find books, and help authors find their footing. I appreciate all reviews.

Georgette's story is Book Two of the *Greenpoint Artists* series. Alanna's story is told in Book One, *Hold Me Tight*, which is currently available. There's also a prequel novella, *Draw Me In*.

Hayley's story, *Give Me Shelter*, will come next, release date to be determined. (Sign up for the newsletter and find out when!)

Georgette and Alanna also appear in *Call Me Saffron*, which takes place in the same Greenpoint, Brooklyn community.

# Draw Me In

Bike messenger/struggling artist Raven Porter and pickle purveyor Finn McKenna have instant chemistry when they meet during a routine delivery, so when Finn discovers her crashing in his empty warehouse later that night, he doesn't throw her out. Instead, he serenades her with his jazz saxophone.

Raven and Finn fit together. Two creative souls, their passions hidden behind sturdy defenses. If they can only let each other in...

## Excerpt:

Finn closed the office door behind him and started downstairs--but paused, catching movement out of the corner of his eye.

Someone was in the warehouse room.

He swung the door open all the way. And stopped, dumbfounded.

A woman swayed in a swath of sunlight, arms outstretched, dancing to music only she could hear. Dark hair swirled with her graceful movements. A T-shirt clung to her curves. Her jeans had holes in both knees and paint stains down the thighs. She was beautiful in an entirely unexpected way--off-kilter and quirky, with dark slashes for eyebrows and a wide, generous mouth, tipped up in a blissful inward smile.

She danced in his loft space like she owned the place.

He stepped into the room, compelled. Wanting and not wanting to break the spell.

She turned, twirling on her toe as if her shoe were a ballet slipper and not a mud-stained work boot. He could tell the moment she saw him. She toppled off her toes and stood flat-footed. "You're Finn McKenna, I'm guessing?"

"And you're...?"

"Raven. I was looking for you. I got distracted." She picked up a box, proffering it.

Right. She must be the courier. The thought was disconcerting, as if she shouldn't have such a prosaic role in life. He took the box. "Where do I sign?"

She handed him her electronic pad, then, as an afterthought, the pen that went with it. As he reached to take it, she flushed. Their fingers grazed—an electric spark like a jolt of attraction—and the pen fell to the floor.

They reached for it at the same time, then both pulled back in a comedy of errors. She grinned at him with a hint of wickedness in the curve of her mouth and the tilt of her slightly pointed chin, and he felt himself smiling back, almost unwillingly. *Mental note: bike couriers can be sexy as hell.*

# Hold Me Tight

Alanna thought she'd never see Miles again. He was her first lover. The boy who broke her heart. But now he's the creative director at a high-profile ad agency and she's an impoverished artist. She needs the job he offers her.

Miles thinks he's gotten over Alanna. Brash, reckless, vivid Alanna. It's been eleven years, after all. When he hires her, he swears to himself that he'll keep away. For his own sake, and for the job: the office has a strict no-fraternizing policy.

Once they start working together, they're drawn to each other, tormented by what they can't have.

And then one sultry summer evening, a citywide blackout gives them an unexpected opportunity.

Tonight, in the dark, they can both pretend she's someone else. Tonight they can be together. A second chance at love, but a risky one.

*Hold Me Tight* won the RWA® Golden Heart for Contemporary Romance.

# Pixel Perfect
## Book One of the Miranda Skye
## Mystery series

Budding photographer Miranda Skye thinks it's going to be an easy gig: return to her eccentric Catskills town, shoot a fancy faculty party at the local college as a favor to her dad, then sit down to a raucous family dinner.

And it *is* easy. Until she stumbles on the body. The one she just happens to capture in her camera's sights. The one that's going to wreak havoc on her father's career if the culprit isn't found, pronto.

The local cops think sexy bad boy Donovan James, aka Miranda's high school nemesis, did the deed. Which should delight her. Except that she has a niggling feeling they're arresting the wrong man.

And for some strange reason, she feels the need to exonerate him.

(And no, that kiss has nothing to do with it.)

(Nothing at all.)

Sign up for my newsletter at www.taliasurova.com to be alerted when *Pixel Perfect* is released.

# Acknowledgments

The fact that this book even exists is all due to Dan Valverde. I was going to put it down and give up before I got started. He talked me through it, brainstorming possible directions it could go and who these people were. When we were done, I said, "Okay, there's a book here." But when I wrote the first draft, I hit another wall. He said, "No, it doesn't need as much of an overhaul as you think," and we talked through the details and permutations. And he was right. He did the job of a developmental editor. A brilliant one. And I'm more grateful than I can express.

I also want to thank my critique partners, Alaya Dawn Johnson and Sonali Dev. I'm the luckiest writer on the planet to have these two brilliant authors in my corner. Also Wendy LaCapra for our walks and her support and great notes. And Leya Evelyn and Sohini Baliga for their invaluable beta reads. And Linda Ingmanson, my terrific copy editor. And my cats, who keep me company when I write, and my son, who usually doesn't. And to lemonade and tea and chocolate, which sustain me as I work. And the Firebirds and Lucky 13s, my beloved writer communities.

And to you, my readers. Thank you.

# About the Author

Talia Surova began her writing career as a screenwriter but switched to prose after she started writing an online journal for fun. This led to writing fiction, which led to writing romance.

She won the Romance Writers of America® Golden Heart Award in 2012 for Hold Me Tight and is a two-time finalist. She was a 2015 RWA RITA finalist for *Call Me Saffron.*

She now lives in New York City, her childhood hometown, with her husband and son.